Curiosities is a thrice annual publication of short speculative fiction in the retropunk subgenres.

In this edition, you will find ten stories from the age of jazz and diesel, with hard boiled detectives, fast talking time travelers, bakelite automatons, body hopping cultists, ambitious aviators, a Tesla powered metropolis, and the Fairy King himself in Weimar Berlin.

Welcome to our fall exhibits of wonders and curiosities.

Curiosities #4 Autumn 2018.
©2018 by Kevin Frost

"Badlands Dentistry"©2018 by Eddie Generous.
"Children of the Coil"©2017 by Sebastien Mantle first appeared in *Stories from the World of Tomorrow* (Darkhouse Books).
"Doppelganger"©2018 by DJ Tyrer.
"Horns of Gold and Hands of Silver" ©2018 by Dimitra Nikolaidou.
"How to Murder a Corpse"©2018 by Brian K. Lowe.
"The Pinch"©2017 by M.A. Smith, first appeared in *Gathering Storm #5*.
"Spirit in the Sky"©2018 by Marlin Bressi.
"The Sultana of Story"©2018 by Jordan Taylor, first appeared in *New Myths #42*.
"This Particular Evening"©2017 by Manuel Royal.
"Two Steps Forward"©2015 by Holly Schofield, first appeared in *Scarecrow* (World Weaver Press).

Cover art: "Do androids......?" ©2018 by Goren Delic deviantart.com/delic.
Ornamental clip art via bomg shutterstock.com/g/bomg.
Flatware clip art via The Old Design Shop olddesignshop.com.

ISBN-13: 978-1-948396-05-9 (Print on Demand)
ISBN-13: 978-1-948396-06-6 (EPUB)
ISBN-13: 978-1-948396-07-3 (iBook)

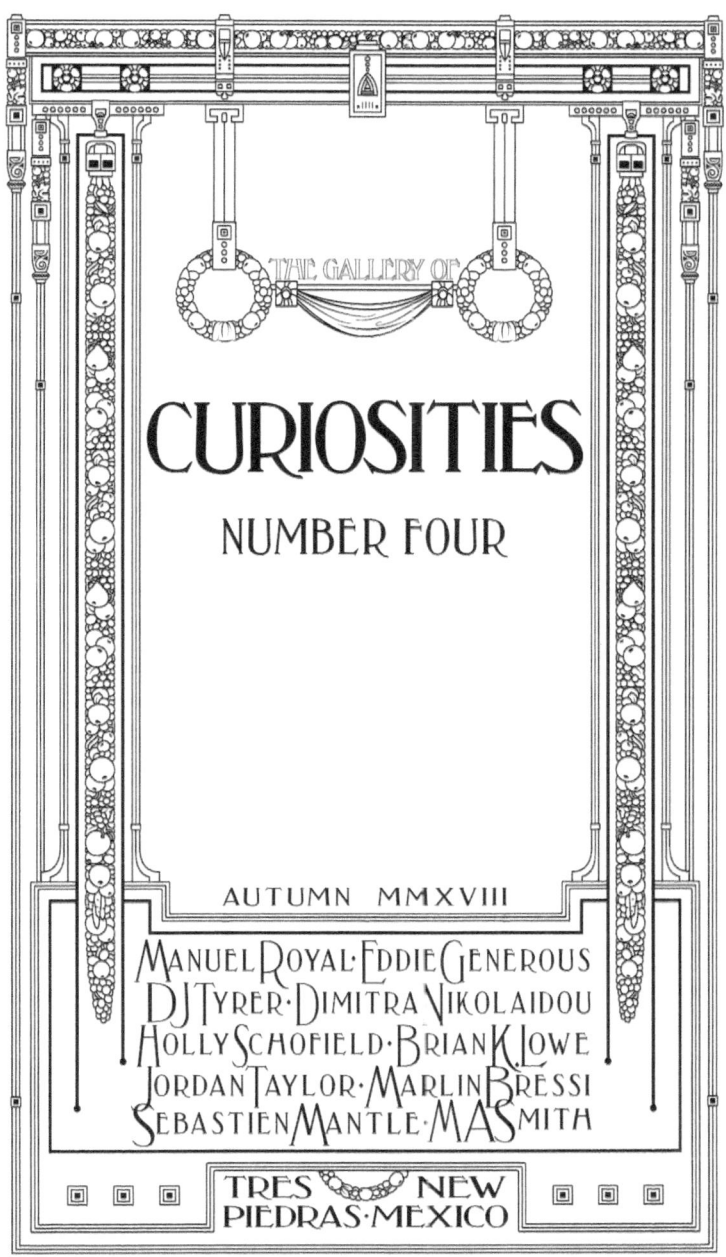

THE GALLERY OF

CURIOSITIES

NUMBER FOUR

AUTUMN MMXVIII

MANUEL ROYAL · EDDIE GENEROUS
DJ TYRER · DIMITRA NIKOLAIDOU
HOLLY SCHOFIELD · BRIAN K. LOWE
JORDAN TAYLOR · MARLIN BRESSI
SEBASTIEN MANTLE · MA SMITH

TRES NEW
PIEDRAS · MEXICO

CONTENTS

My mother had beautiful books when she was a child.

Her parents came of age in the late 1920s. I found their youthful photos when it was time to clean out their house. But I never found those books.

Ken was in Electrical Engineering at the University of Utah. He and his best friend Nishi made marvels and played pranks. They drove a roadster by remote control in a parade, and every time it paused everyone had to come and look inside to verify that no one was hiding on the floorboards. He had a bright future ahead of him as a radioman, or would have, if not for the fact that he graduated in 1929.

Nishi went back to Japan. Ken went back to Wyoming and did day labor for the railroad. I always remembered him as a radioman. He had a little radio repair shop in Rock Springs. Every Friday night the people would come around and stand in the dust out front to hear the boxing match broadcast over the loudspeakers he had bolted to the side of the building.

Upstairs from the shop was a brothel. One time the girls asked him to come up and fix their radio. He dashed up, brought it back down to the shop, and hoped like hell no one had seen him go up there. Especially Izetta.

From looking at their photographs, I imagine that Ken and Izetta were the slickest young couple in all of Wyoming. In one picture he is in overalls along a railroad track, leaning on a shovel, "pretending to work" wrote Izetta in white photo album ink. In the next, they are smiling into the camera lens, eyes full of mischief, he in a dark suit with wide lapels, she in a cloche hat and dress coat with lush fur cuffs and collars. They are stopped on the side of a road somewhere, next to a fairly shiny roadster, shadows long. There's a lot of dirt. They might grown up podunk, but they had an eye to be city slickers.

They moved to San Francisco and bought a new art deco stucco with a drive-in basement, way up on a hill. Very modern for the era. It even had a hide-a-way telephone sconce, with a fold out shelf that had a compart-ment for the phone book. His claim to fame was building the first FM radio station on the west coast.

I don't know what he did during the war. He told someone once, but then they didn't publish, and he didn't want to go through the whole trouble of ever anyone else again. I never saw any evidence of military service. What ever he did, I'm sure it had something to do with commun-ications, and I can't help but wonder if Nishi was doing the same thing on his side of the Pacific. We always had to wait until the football games were over to eat our New Year's Day dinners, as Ken was the one who made sure folks got to see the Rose Bowl in Hawaii. Maybe that is a clue.

Ken only met Nishi once more in his life, during the 1980s, for lunch. He belonged to a powerful old family, and no doubt had had an impressive career.

When Ken and Izetta were presented with grand-children, they left out their daughter's childhood things to keep us occupied while they talked of adult things. They had had *excellent* taste in toys and books. My own belongings of the mid-1960s looked flat and shallow by comparison.

I suppose this is why I have had a hard time warming up to dieselpunk, as these visits put much of the early 20th century into my expanded memory. I don't have enough separation from the era to provide the escapism I prefer in my leisure reading. But, as there were a couple of diesel-powered orphans in our production pile that didn't sit right next to the steampunk stories, we put an emphasis on the early part of the 20th century during our final reading session of the year so we could fill an issue.

What struck me most about this set was a distinctive voice. There's a jazzy rhythm, a sense of optimism, that even if times were bad, there was a better world ahead. Detective stories were the most popular theme that came in. We picked three for this volume, one set just after the Great War, and two in the classic *noire* voice. The first deals with vampires in Los Angeles, and the other, the only truly retro-futurist piece in this volume, is set in a Tesla-powered version of New York City.

Missing from this volume is World War Two. The voices of those stories were very different than those of the peace-time stories, so we decided to give a 'soft' rejection with an invite to resubmit, and penciled in a WW2 themed issue in 2019. The war does loom in the background here, as a foreshadowing of what is to come after Weimar Berlin, a mention of refugee ships arriving in America, and another mention that puts it in memory. Also missing from this volume is Madeleine Swann's excellent 1920s flapper tale which, after much back and forthing in the editing room, was decided to be more of a horror story. Next time, Madeleine, promise.

And if you happen to have a certain copy of *East of the Sun and West of the Moon,* the one with the north wind holding out his black deco wings above a frothy sea, I want it. I've owned many versions, but never have I found one that was as beautiful as the one my mother had when she was a child.

Kevin Frost
Tres Piedras, New Mexico
November 2018

THIS PARTICULAR EVENING

MANUEL ROYAL

THIS PARTICULAR EVENING in, oh, 1927, a nice mild Autumn evening it is, I am standing on Broadway, standing and musing. All 'round my little paved isle of musings, the 1927 clockpunchers are milling about with nary a clue in regards their own existence, as always.

As I am standing there with no particular plans, which is how I like it, who but Joey Epilogue comes up to me from nowhere and at once I discern Joey is gloomy as a thundercloud.

Now it is only human nature that one heart shall call out to another heart, or sometimes it is two or three hearts, and there are certainly other red-blooded organs to be considered as well. Be that as it may, it is known to one and all in the Circuit that Joey Epilogue and Quick Dip Bitsy are forever in love and out of love, smashing together and breaking up with much noise and tears, then leaping back into the fray again in a big messy romantic tangle.

For a heady month here (Justinian's Constantinople), a

delir-ious week there (1519, Tenochtitlan) they are hot and heavy and dancing a tango in Heaven, but then again many another time she is cold as ice (1871, Chicago on fire) or he is on a spiteful bender and can in no wise be pleased for all of Bitsy's lovey-dovey ministrations (1666, London on fire).

Now both Bitsy and Joey have a mischievous bent, which is known all 'round the Circuit. Once upon a time Bitsy gets quasi-elected to the 2087 Eastern Autonomy Cabinet so she can watch the Engram Crisis, and once upon another time in 1150-some-thing Joey stumbles backwards into supposed godhead, finding himself worshiped as such on some rocky island. Between the two of them they bend many a rule, not too much, no more than a baker bends a pretzel. (Mulberry Street, 1912, look for Otto Voos' pushcart, for therein lie the best pretzels found in the City of New York at any time.)

But such incidents and varied peccadillos are not the cause of trouble betwixt Joey and Bitsy. No. Anyone—that is, anyone who is not Bitsy or Joey—can see that they are much too much alike to be together. They yank and shove each other, attract and repulse. They get crazy, they forget every guideline of polite behavior whenever they clap eyes on each other. (Such as for instance Dropping-In on them-selves and doubling down in public. A couple dozen of the crowd at Queen's Erlanger Theater concert in Philly in 1975 are Joey and Bitsy. After the concert they all fill up a suite at the Loews and do things that are not in the dictionary.)

But this particular evening as I enjoy a bit of 1927, I happen to know Bitsy is meanwhile in 1755 Lisbon taking in the earth-quake, so while Joey Epilogue darts among the square black cars of 1927 I am curious regarding the cause of his distress. But it is no kind of a mystery why he seeks me out: Joey needs an ear and a shoulder and a rider on some other fellow's bar tab.

Sure enough, Joey at once touches me for a drink, which is fine because Prohibition New York is my favorite spot for tippling. There are within an easy walk numerous speakeasies that serve decent liquor and have decent bartenders and are full of indecent patrons. Clockpunchers they may be, and therefore as much shadow as substance, but they are companionable shadows enjoying the fellowship known only to a gathering of lawbreakers, and that is good enough for me.

Meanwhile, 2044 is my least favorite time to even attempt to find a friendly drink anywhere in New York, city or state, for obvious reasons.

Joey is down at the mouth and ready to spill, so like a gent I pry open my purse, and soon a sturdy barman is pouring the juice in my glass a stingy ounce at a time and Joey is pouring his troubles into my ear by the bucketful.

"It is Bitsy," he says. "We are on the outs now and again, and that much I can live with, but this time I am afraid it is over for good and all. You must help me fix this."

Now once in 1692 Salem Village I must make Joey Epilogue watch a witch hanging to convince him they do not burn witches in 17th century America. So with Joey one must show, not tell, to convey simple facts. With not-so-simple facts, one must sell him on repeat performances.

One time, just for example, Joey takes a notion to go and save President Garfield from his normally scheduled assassination. There is nothing for it but we must intercept Charles Guiteau and drop him, plop! in the Potomac, then Drop-In at the 1884 election. Joey expects to see Garfield winning a second term, and is singularly disgruntled to find that Garfield is indeed three years dead and Chester Arthur is soon to be out of a job, defeated by Grover Cleveland.

Yet Joey has got the stubborns and is raring for another

try, and so we go catch Guiteau in 1860 on his way to Oneida and we see to it he gets run over by a train. You will not be surprised that when we stop in 1882, Garfield, just as stubborn, continues to have died.

Does Joey Epilogue give up on Garfield and Guiteau and Guiteau's gun? He does not.

In 1841 Freeport, Illinois, we burn to ashes the Guiteau family home whilst Mama Guiteau is therein birthing little baby Charles, and then we hop to 1881 and—yes, that is right—we watch Guiteau, whole and hale and unburnt, pump two bullets into Garfield from behind. This is profound and instructive, both for Joey and for Garfield.

Joey and I walk up for a good look at fat bleeding Garfield and then go and waste much good drinking time in a high-class den of sin as I take advantage of the multiple mirrors to try and explain that we on the Circuit, and all the poor oblivious clock-punchers we intercept, and indeed the whole sad world we see at any point along the Throughline, are all and only reflections of reflections, infinitely close to immutable reality but never one with it. You cannot alter or even leave a lasting mark on a single heartbreaking twist or ludicrous curve along the Through-line. It is as it is. And that is why we observe and absorb, and enjoy the spectacle, and do not waste our energies a-meddling.

I say to Joey, "Joey, my lad, you and I upon the Circuit may hear the unending strings of reality humming and thrumming, but we can never in no wise touch them, however much we might shout against their echo." Says I. (Such are the metaphors one comes up with on a long night in an unlawful brass-and-velvet saloon and bordello.)

At last Joey's incandescent bulb sparks up, and he vows to no more strive at unwriting the written record. Also, soon thereafter Joey first meets Quick Dip Bitsy and from then on she is the flame and he is the moth, or perhaps they are both moths and both fire, mutually flaming and flapping, to use a metaphor I locate one evening in a bottle of absinthe while peacefully enjoying the Siege of Paris.

But this particular Prohibition evening, Joey is hurting, and Bitsy is gone off, and that is all his brain has room for and he is not in the market for any gold coins of wisdom I may toss his way in our friendly neighborhood speakeasy. Many and many another evening, all around the Circuit, here and there one-dimensionally along the Throughline, in many lands and climes, Joey pines and pains and works the problem, and Joey never does and never will get it (and nor do any of us wise and wizened old souls) in his brain and in the old tick-tock, that Bitsy is not, nor is any lover or would-be lover or once-was lover, a problem, a puzzle, a mechanical difficulty that one may simply work at until one solves it—nondestructively, that is to say.

We of all and any genders, tripping gaily about the Circuit or plodding antwise down the Throughline, we are all alike foolish in love, all alike simple saps haplessly floundering and helpless against desire and loss, for much as we dream of scratching out this shameful episode here or revising that noble failure there, old Lady Fate, working at her loom with just that one long thread, will have her way, and you may as well go try and save Garfield as try and make someone keep loving you when their heart no longer ticks and tocks for you.

All of which I say out loud, not that Joey is cognizant or receptive. No, Joey's eyes are glazed and fixed on a point maybe eight feet in front of him, and Joey says to me: "It is not that at all, for Bitsy tells me last night in old Byzantium that she loves me as steady as the stars in their courses. Verily she digs me the most, and I'll not gainsay her, for

Quick Dip Bitsy's word is as good as any and better than most."

"So what then," ask I, "is the problem betwixt you pair?"

"Bitsy is jawing with the Empress Theodora at the chariot races, and while I do not exactly lend them both ears, I do hear the subject of marriage coming up. So I figure Bitsy is giving the Empress her two cents as re how to handle Emperor Justinian, but now I am thinking she must be getting a nickel change back because that night while we are watching the Nika riots get heated up, Bitsy tells me nothing will do but that we must make it official. Ring on the finger."

Now those of us on the Circuit tend to be free and easy types and unfettered by bonds of matrimony. For with the Throughline spun silklike through all of written history, up and down, side to side, providing limitless opportunities for fun and frolic with clockpunching shadow people, and with Drop-ins by their 'pataphysical nature being very individual experiences, we are not commonly inclined to pledge devotion to the ones with whom we are now and then comfortably inclined.

I open my mouth to say all of this to Joey Epilogue, when what but he pulls out of his pants pocket a little velvet box, and opening that box shows me a very goldish and glittery ring, which I can see right off is just the sort of sparkly and splendid thing Quick Dip Bitsy would enjoy and cherish. All the more so since it is surely filched from some queenly tomb and will appeal to Bitsy's acquisitive nature.

Joey says, "So Bitsy is handing me the old ultimatum. And not only that, it is not enough I must steal a ring from Juana la Loca because she is the same ring size. No, Bitsy tells me she is roaming here and there on the Circuit, Dropping-In at any intersect on the Throughline takes her fancy, leaving me not a clue, and I must find her somehow or I can go chase my tail and if so we are splitsville because it is Fate."

I do not mention the obvious solution to this conundrum, i.e., walking away and enjoying the near-limitless other possibilities offered by life on the Circuit, knowing Joey Epilogue as I do, for he will not listen to anything that does not lay a path for him to hoof back to Bitsy's side, or possibly Bitsy's front.

Joey is even asking the clockpuncher tending bar what he should do, and indeed maybe this is one of the situations, even disregarding the highly esoteric physics, metaphysics, and 'pata-physics involved, in which a bartender of any era might have as much wisdom as the most seasoned Circuit rider.

Indeed, the barman, making my drink, does not even look up from his sacred ministrations, but he says: "Look here, Brother, if you are happier having the miseries with this doll than you are on your lonesome, then you are a lost bunny and must do whatever is called for to put that manacle on her." Which is enough to give Joey Epilogue a dose of the lovelorn stubborns. Joey excuses himself to the Gents' and is back while I am still sipping my Rock & Rye. I know he is Dropping-In here and there and everywhere upon the Throughline, for he is worn and sore and wearing different clothes and somewhat older in the face than when he went to the Gents.'

"It is a sissifying task!" he cries, by which he means Sisyphean, or possibly he means what he says. "I am all over Creation looking for that woman, and by God it is exhausting. I am an expert now on every earthquake since Babylon, for as you know Bitsy loves to feel the ground shake. But she is not there, or then, no matter where or when I am on the hunt. Her last words to me are as a mockery, for she is saying, 'Joey, show me that you do not give up easy.' Give up easy! However am I to find a woman who is not where she should surely be?"

During Joey Epilogue's epic five minutes in the Gents' I have troubled to learn the name of the shadow-man clockpuncher behind the bar, and it is Elroy. I tap the rim of my glass, and Elroy is prompt to tend to the emptiness within it, but with such a thoughtful look on his puss that I ask him, "What is the word, Elroy?" and he lays an elbow down on the bar and leans well in.

"Brother," he says to Joey, "My whole life, I know two things about dolls. One is, you must take them at their word. Two is, no matter what you think they should be doing, they are doing what the Hell they feel like doing."

Now Elroy sets my fresh and tasty Rock & Rye on the bar, but I have not so much as a sip thereof because Joey Epilogue grabs my lapel and drags me bodily back into the Gents' with him, and strike me pink if we are not immediately Dropping-In on a warm summer Washington, D.C. day in 1881, stepping lively in a train depot that feels familiar as a favorite vacation spot because over there is President James Garfield going into the waiting room to wait for his train to Williams College, and yonder comes the fatedly murderous Charles Guiteau, but not a single eye does Joey Epilogue have for the unfolding historical violence tableau because standing squarely between us and the soon-to-be action is a little black-haired twist in a summer frock, none other than Quick Dip Bitsy. What does Joey do but drop to a knee in front of her right there, and pops open his little velvet box just as the first shot booms.

Bitsy has her arms around Joey before the second shot, and the two of them are off! I am hearing later that they are married by a Judge Joseph Crater.

Needless to say, the torrid twosome, all of time at their disposal but clearly prioritizing how they use it, have not a moment to spare for a task as pedestrian as thanking their older and wiser friend, nay benefactor and educator.

I have had enough of both romantic mania and assassination for one evening, and decide to return to my neglected Prohibition cocktail, but first I stroll up to have one last look at poor prostrate President Garfield, who is surrounded by a crowd and is bleeding but remarkably calm in that he is unconscious.

I tell him, "Mister President, it is a pity that you have got two months of suffering ahead of you. But let me tell you, that is *nothing* compared to the ordeal that Joey Epilogue has just volunteered for!"

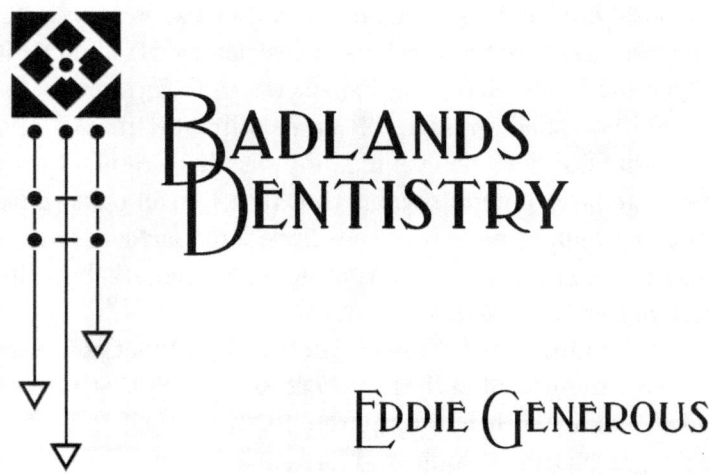

BADLANDS DENTISTRY

EDDIE GENEROUS

THE BONES OF GIANT LIZARDS were the kind of novelty that kept folks interested, but the unearthed coal kept them fed.

It was 1915 and the town of Drumheller had a doctor, a sheriff, two deputies, and two saloons. A Catholic church had room for the devout as well as all those who might make it next week. Drumheller also had a dentist.

Bag in hand, the dentist rushed between the loose dunes of sand. Through a valley of crumbling yellow rock formations carved by a two and a half billion year history of spilled lava, glacial movements, and some very hard times more recently, the clapboard home had all the markings of trouble. The dentist worried that he'd chased this boy into another situation with Indians. Always on the run was no way for a dentist, or his family, to exist.

"Come on, Mama's got it bad."

Unconventional was something a dentist with a good reputation and coins jangling in his pocket had the opportunity to complain about. Mr. Daniel Lewis shut his mouth and followed the boy.

The door of the tiny rundown home had a tin sign for White Rose Motor Oil tacked to its side. Below, spider web cracks reached for edges. Door open, the dentist staggered a step. The lived-in stink of summer was everywhere: body odor, bacon grease, and old coal.

The boy's mother, Laura Wilson, lay on a threadbare sofa, a damp towel over her forehead.

"Have you got a lamp?" Lewis asked, setting his bag on a kitchen table, cluttered with dirty dishes and candle nubbins.

"Pa don't like us to waste it during daytime. He'll be back any day now."

"This is important, and fetch me some fresh water in a clean bucket. Get your brothers to help."

"They's girls," the boy said and waved to the trio standing in a shadowy corner by the fireplace. They dressed identically in ruddy shirts and short pants held up with twine suspenders. Heads shaved.

"Oh," Lewis said.

"Had lice," Her words sounded as if she had a mouth full of acorns.

"Come on over to the table and let me have a look."

She sat up, letting the cloth fall. Her expression was agony, her mouth emitted a continual low-level yowl. The strain had her eyes bloodshot.

The dentist helped her to a seat and ordered an open mouth. Swelling bubbled in a great yellow bulge out from her lower gums. It was another abscess and sweat ran. In dentistry, it was the shock of pain that killed folks as much as anything else—supposing a body doesn't wait out an infection to kill them in slow torment first.

Morphine was an option, but that was trouble. It was also expensive and running low. However, if ever there was a time to use it, this was it. He pulled the bottle from the bag.

"Don't gimme none of that!"

"This is for the pain."

"I know what it is. Kill't my father."

The kids charged back into the home with a steel bucket full of cloudy, yellowy water.

Their mother saw this and said, "Where's the well bucket?"

One of the three girls said, "Fell in after Mary let loose the rope."

"Was you!" another said.

The boy stepped in next with an oil lamp.

"Boy, you stand right here," Lewis said, moving the boy in place, "and hold that lamp steady. Girls, bring me that water and fetch me some clean rags and cloths."

"Mama ain't done no wash," the boy said.

"Clean-ish will have to do, now hurry." There was a lip-smeared water glass on the table. Lewis dunked it in the bucket, set it aside full. The girls returned with clothes in various stages of filth. "Thanks."

The cleanest of the clothes, a faded red checker, went into the bucket and came out sopping. Lewis retrieved a scalpel from his bag.

"Open wide. This will sting something terrible."

Tears began to fall, but Laura dutifully opened her mouth. The blade pierced the swelling and greenish fluid poured free. The woman screamed, her hands white-knuckling the sides of the chair seat.

As he pulled out the scalpel, the woman's jawed snapped shut.

"Open!"

She did and while she swallowed the horrid stuff, Lewis dabbed the rag gently against the loose, harried flesh. That done, he straightened up. The woman looked better already. In fact, she looked almost too much better.

Lewis leaned forward, fearing shock. "Ma'am, you still with me?"

"That's wonderful. I can't feel a thing in my mouth, still tastes bad. Can I drink?"

The dentist straightened and nodded to the glass. She drank it back and smiled further.

"I can't feel my mouth at all."

"What?"

"It's gone, so is the pain."

She was smiling. Odd. The dentist ordered her to open up and prodded the worrying spot. She did not flinch. A fortunate man might complain of the mystery of good luck, but Lewis knew better.

He explained cleaning with salt and soapsuds. He explained the importance of brushing and that the kids needed their teeth cleaned too.

She nodded. The dentist was her god right then.

Before Lewis left, he said to the girls, "Show me where you got that water."

Back a path, into the bush, through a wall of blackflies, they came upon a sandy opening in the forest. "Well, I'll be." It was the most incredible thing Lewis had ever seen.

The skull was bigger than any animal to ride Noah's Ark. It was complete and imprinted nearly flat in stone, the size of a covered wagon. From the eyehole of the petrified dinosaur, yellowy water sat in a trickling pool. It was the same water that was in the bucket.

A finger went in, it was warm, and then touched his tongue. Almost instantly, the dentist's tongue numbed at the source point.

Word got around of a dentist named Moody practicing on the west coast, using sedatives and numbing fluids.

When word of a dentist gets anywhere beyond the outskirts of his practice, good chance it's because of a breakthrough or a monumental screw-up. Breakthroughs equal handsome pockets and screw-ups, well, Lewis knew about those as it was.

He returned to his tiny rental home and found his wife, Emily, in the living room, humming along with their phonograph while it spun The Pink Lady original cast recording. She had her eyes closed and Lewis was almost certain she tried to imagine what it looked like on Broadway. Once the song ended, he told Emily of the peculiar situation.

Her mental cogs turned after he'd summed the fame of the Vancouver dentist. Then, the children gathered round while their mother told tales of how their father would have them living in a real city, with dress shops and candy shops, living how they should be living, and soon. She told them they'd be front and center, basking in the afterglow of Broadway's bright lights.

⤛⚬ ⚬⤜

"Hello there," Laura said. "I didn't think I needed you to come back, little pained, but not too bad."

"Ma'am, is your husband home today?" Lewis said.

The woman stepped out and closed the door behind her. "That man went north for gold and ain't never coming back. The kids don't underst—"

Lewis interrupted, "Say nothing more. I have a proposition for you."

They worked out a deal. He tested the water on the children. They did not squirm or worry, did not move a bit as he scraped and scratched the crud from their teeth. That water was a miracle.

It was a week gone and the dentist poured the last

pennies he had into paper and ink. He and Emily wrote flyers, one hundred in all.

FREE GENERAL DENTAL CHECK-UP

AVOID COSTLY REPAIRS LATER

TEETH CLEANING 50¢

MINOR SURGERY $2

MAJOR SURGERY $5

TEETH CLEANING FREE FOR CHILDREN WITH ADULT CLEANING

ONE DAY ONLY 5AM TO 10PM IN THE OFFICE OF

MR. LEWIS: DENTIST

The children helped hand out the flyers, but only one flyer came to matter. Mr. Alvin Welling was not a man of dental luck and he knew the pain and the time that it wasted. Coal miners with happy mouths equalled managers with happy bosses in the city. He ordered the employees to take the day and tend to their oral hygiene.

There were a dozen or so heads more than three hundred in Drumheller and every last one of them showed up. Mrs. Lewis owner of the magic well, helped with cleaning. The townsfolk swished and rinsed the magic water.

By the end of the longest day since escaping the torments of the Frog Lake tribe—long in all the right ways this time—Lewis' pockets jangled heavy. His business partner, as limited as her share was, was happy. Most importantly, his wife and kids might just meet those pipedreams of big city living.

The following day, he put in an order for new tools from the hardware store and a new horse wagon to take his practice on the road.

The wagon was royal blue with silver lettering. Lewis had eyes every bit as big as his wife had, though tinted differently. He'd get here away from the dust and nothingness and he'd be celebrity. A world famous dentist.

><≡   ≡><

"Don't you think you'd best do the kids?" Emily said two days after the big day.

The family had good clean teeth, but they could always be cleaner. Lewis splashed the magic water into their mouths one at a time and got busy. They smiled wide, numb on magic water.

"How about you?" Emily asked, she was a great assistant, but when it came to the dentist himself, her wielding the tools meant something else. "Want to try it with the stuff?"

He shook his head, that single dab was all he'd ever have. There was a reason dentistry took his heart at a young age and a big part of that was the agonizing erection he'd had while his childhood dentist yanked a sideways molar from the back of his mouth. He'd begun to look into things, testing if it was the images, the touch, even pain in general, but it was none of that. The invasive under layer ache of dental work was an elixir to his loins.

Eventually it was Emily who had helped hone this knowledge.

She closed the door, lowered her knickers beneath her dress, picked up a scraper, opened Lewis' pants, and sat on his lap to clean his teeth.

><≡   ≡><

A full week after the big day, the Lewis family sat at the base of natural earthen upraise of crust. Emily explained that the different colors in the soil meant different centuries. She explained that the porous stones might not be stones at all and that scientists collected them to put them together. "Dinosaur bones, from before God put people on the Earth," Emily said as she bit into a piece of raisin bread. "Now dinosaurs were enormous, so each bone you fit into your hand might be the same kind of bo—Ouch!" A seed had connected with a weakened spot of an eyetooth. She held her face.

"Uh oh," Lewis said. "Open up."

On the yellow knit blanket, amid the swarming blackflies, and the dinosaur bone pieces, from particle to whole, the dentist assessed his patient's mouth.

"You've cracked it. We'll need to watch it. Does it hurt?"

Emily nodded.

"Susan, fetch some of that magic water."

Thirty-three days after the big day, and forty-one days after the initial discovery, the dentist and his wife stood in the office, looking at a map. The idea was to make the biggest bang possible on a much grander scale than what Drumheller had to offer. Calgary was good, but Vancouver would be better. Better yet would be south of the border: Spokane, Seattle, Portland.

"Calgary first," Emily said, using a red pencil on the map. "Then see, we go south and west."

Lewis kissed the part of hair on Emily's scalp. She was ambitious and knew what she wanted. It was his job to be the gateway for her journey. His becoming famous didn't hurt if it happened along the way.

It was twelve days prior to the scheduled leave. He stared in the mirror, looking at the tip of his tongue. A spot twice the size of typically enlarged papillae had become like a stone, but seemed to weigh less than other parts of his tongue. There was no feeling in the spot. He chewed it, off and on.

He had a job on a horse. It wasn't the norm, but the water worked on equine as well as human, and money was money. The horse had broken tooth that had made it irritable and a risk to ride. The tooth came out of the numbed mouth and a boy came running around to the back of the office.

"Mr. Lewis, it's Mama!" he said and broke away.

The old woman holding the horse's reins rolled her eyes. "I don't think I'd have the patience for your occupation, good sir."

"Excuse me. If you'd like to settle up, my wife is inside." The woman nodded and Lewis climbed atop the bare back of his own horse.

The boy was at the side of the home, hopping up and down, excited. His eyes terrified. "Come, quick!"

Much as it had been on his first visit, Laura lay flat on the sofa. Her arm dangling to the floor. Two things were different: there was no cloth over her face, and the texture of her flesh was wrong.

The protrusion on the tip of the dentist's tongue clicked against his teeth. And a second time. And a third, as if offering a clue. He approached and touched the woman. She was cool, dry, and pale yellow. The skin was papery, stretched over clean, thick bone.

Lewis shook her, trying to connect the sense and impossibility into a notion of reality. "Wake up. Wake up."

The dangling arm fell off and the girls screamed in harmony. The boy leapt onto the dentist's back. He swung and then scratched, trailing filthy boy-claws along the dentist's scalp. "I'll kill you! You hurt Mama!"

Spinning, Lewis sent the skinny child rocketing against

the water stained wallpaper by the fireplace. "Calm now and let me figure this out."

Through a slight gap in her throat, the dentist pushed a finger, tearing the papery flesh. Beneath it felt bone-like. She wasn't a skeleton. Her body had become bone, the muscles, the tendons, the fluids. Bone.

He picked up the arm and clicked it back in place like a key in a keyhole. "See, all better. She just needs rest. But it also needs to remain a secret." The hard nub on his tongue clicked again, nailing an idea that he didn't dare express just yet. "So, you, boy, go tell my wife I need to spend the evening with a sick patient, but tell her not to panic. Got it?"

The boy stood, rubbed his elbow. Tear streaks uglied his dirty cheeks.

It was a night long and difficult. When the sun arose, the wait continued. The children whined and moaned, asking relentlessly how long until their mother awoke.

The eldest girl came first. One minute she was a nagging bundle of tears, the next she was a stiffening visage. Her face wore a scowl of discomfort. She slipped sideways. The boy started abrading the dentist, not connecting that he was next.

A tiny, boyish fist connected with Lewis' face. The dentist latched on and hugged the child, whispering, "It's not my fault. It's not my fault."

Once the boy turned, Lewis apologized, leaving the last two girls in the living room, wailing and cradling their boney siblings and mother.

Watching Lewis pack a suitcase, Emily, curious but willing, asked, "A vacation, right before you leave?"

"Sure, out of town before we hit the road for pure

business. Be a secret getaway."

They took the wagon, loading the camping gear alongside the dental supplies. They slept in the woods, had campfires, sang Broadway tunes. The dentist and his business muse made love.

They returned to Drumheller to find a ghost town.

"I want you to stay inside. I'll find out what's going on."

The trees whispered in the wind and Lewis stood over the well of all of recent hopes and dreams, peering at the yellowy pool at the center of the eye of a hundred million years dead beast. He came to a conclusion and dipped a cup into the liquid. He stared deep into his cloudy reflection, imaging a future.

"Everyone's sick. A flu, many dead. All's shut-in, we ought to do the same. Can't leave lest we're carriers."

Shocked and terrified, Emily said, "Gosh, we should've stayed away another week."

Lewis played with his kids and held his wife. Time was so very short.

Over the course of a day that passed much too quickly, the kids became bone renditions of themselves. Laura wailed and thrashed about the home. Her time was not far away.

Lewis cut off the tip of his tongue. Emily watched him do and understood then. "When did you know?"

"When Laura went. It's fifty-two days from impact to metamorphosis."

"What is?"

"The magic water."

"But I... Dear God."

"It's not my fault," he said and believed it too. If he didn't believe it, he would've drank his fill from the pool.

People hid valuables all over homes. Lewis knew that. The office safe at the mine was slim, unfortunately. There wasn't enough to take off, start anew in the lap of luxury, have the kind of life he deserved.

He'd considered contacting the government, sell the water to the Allied Troops and solve the Germans once and for all. It was a noble thought, but suggested complicity in the demise of an entire town.

He'd had a vision. With a shovel and spade, with a chisel and hammer, Lewis got to work. Just in case his idea was a bust, he filled thirty-nine emptied liquor bottles with the yellowy water and headed east.

The dentist was no longer a dentist and the last time he was this nervous was while watching a Frog Lake elder succumb to abscess induced shock. Sweat sprouted from his neck, soaking into the crisp collar of his Oxford and the wool collar of his suit jacket.

The room hushed. The thick red curtain rose, lights shined on the stage. The symphony hidden in the shadows between the crowd and the stage came to life. Lewis looked at his family under the bright lights. They danced beautifully on strings. His wife dressed in finery she'd never known before.

The music changed and the dancing became erratic. Stomping out from the wings were the skeletal dancers, creations of Lewis' dentistry, abhorrent conglomerations, abominations to awe the ticket holders: bone people that clacked and swung like marionettes with extended jaws and rows upon rows of teeth, so many teeth.

The crowd gasped.

The music played.

Lewis grinned and cried. They'd made it to New York after all. His family had Broadway. And he had teeth.

DOPPELGANGER

DJ TYRER

IT WAS THREE YEARS after the Great War ended that Major John McKintosh (ret.) died, having spent the intervening period in a coma.

"He was hit by a shell and took a piece of shrapnel to his head." Anne McKintosh, the Major's widow, sighed. "He never recovered."

Frank Issland nodded. "You have my sympathies. How can I help you? Tracing an old comrade or an heir?" He had returned from the mud and blood of Flanders to begin work as a private detective for the new decade.

Mrs. McKintosh took a breath, clearly considering what to say. "If only it were something as simple as that."

"I don't understand. Did he commit a crime?"

"I...I don't think so." She pursed her lips. "My husband has been seen since the funeral."

"Sorry? Did you say, seen? Seen, as in alive?"

She nodded. "And, before. That is what I want you to investigate."

"Whether he is alive? Do you believe he faked his death? That he was only pretending to be in a coma?"

"Well, that is the question, Mr. Issland. I always thought people were mistaken when they said they had seen my husband. It is, after all, not uncommon for one to see a person who looks a little like someone you know. Then, when people who knew him well saw him after he died, I thought it most likely they were misled by grief. But, then, on a trip to London, I saw him myself."

"Could that not have been a product of grief?"

Mrs. McKintosh shook her head. "As much as I wish I could say it were, I cannot believe it. It was either my husband, alive, or his exact twin. It was at that moment I remembered all the times people said they saw him and...and I began to wonder...could it be?"

Frank studied the woman who was sitting opposite him. Her expression was a mixture of sincerity and doubt.

"You want me to discover the truth? Even if it reveals something you may not wish to hear?"

"I need to know: Is my husband dead or have I, somehow, been fooled? All else that might flow from that is merely decoration. I cannot conceive a good reason for him to have misled me, so, if he is alive..." She left the thought unfinished.

"Very well." Frank took out a notebook. "I will need the names and addresses of everyone who saw him, as best you can recall, and every detail you can remember of the time you saw him in London."

She nodded and began to supply them.

The legwork of contacting witnesses was tedious, but a pattern did emerge with many of the sightings being in the same area of London where the widow had seen her husband. Frank was satisfied that, whether the Major was in his grave, he or someone who looked very much like him was to be found.

"The obvious step would be to exhume the body."

Mrs. McKintosh nodded slowly. "I will arrange it."

"In the meantime, may I look through your husband's papers and effects?"

"Of course."

She led him from the drawing room to an office. Several bookshelves were empty.

"It is as my husband left it, before he went to war; save that I was forced to sell many of his books to fund his care. There were some quite rare volumes."

She turned and said, "I will leave you to it," as she left the room.

There was all the usual paperwork Frank would have expected, none of it hinting at anything untoward. Then, he opened a drawer of the dark-wood writing desk and took out a blue-bound diary. Frank opened it and was surprised to see it was written in an alphabet he didn't recognise.

He went to find Mrs. McKintosh and asked her about it.

"I'm not sure what it is. John spent some time in India, perhaps it is from there."

"He was in the army there?"

"No, this was when he was a child and young man, growing up. His aunt took care of him for a time."

"Why was she out there?"

"Oh, she was one of those Theosophists."

"Hmm. I would like to show this book to a friend of mine; he might be able to translate it."

She nodded. "Do."

There was a slight drizzle slowly turning the earth to mud as they stood about the open grave in the churchyard. The undertaker opened the coffin to reveal a desiccated corpse that, Frank thought, looked like the man in the photographs of John McKintosh he had seen. Mrs. McKintosh gasped and looked away.

"It's him," said the gravedigger.

"Reseal it." Frank turned to the undertaker. "Transport it to Doctor Reed."

Reed was the physician who had examined McKintosh in life and would confirm if it was his body. Frank had had an associate look into the doctor's background and was satisfied he was honest and unlikely to be involved in any conspiracy. Soon, they would know...

Frank walked with Mrs. McKintosh from the churchyard back towards her house on the outskirts of the village.

"You said you sold the books from his study?"

"Yes; to a dealer, in London."

"They were rare? What subject?"

"They were ones he inherited from his aunt, ones with odd titles in Latin and Greek and eastern tongues. Theosophical, I would assume."

"Do you have a copy of the bill of sale?"

"I believe so."

"I would like to see it."

Frank dropped the telephone receiver back into the cradle and set it back on the desk, then massaged his brows. The device was rapidly becoming a necessity in his line of business, but it did seem to speed bad news his way.

Prior to the telephone call from Doctor Reed, Frank

had been certain he had solved the case. He had copied the address from the bill of sale and checked its location, which was in the vicinity of where Mrs. McKintosh and others had seen her husband. It had seemed obvious. Then, the doctor had called to confirm the corpse was that of his late patient.

"It doesn't make any sense..." He kept rubbing his temples.

Was the doctor lying? Or, was it all just a bizarre coincidence? The body certainly had looked like McKintosh...He couldn't see any answer now, but the obvious.

Frank picked the telephone up once more and placed a call to his friend.

"Ah, Henderson, Issland here."

"Well timed, old man," Henderson interjected before he could speak. "I was just about to call you..."

"You translated it?"

"Yes."

"Sorry to have wasted your time..."

"No, indeed; it was fascinating."

"Oh, in what way?"

"The fellow had been researching certain passages from the *Krypticon* of Silander in light of little-known Hindu beliefs and was convinced he had achieved the ability to create a thought-form. Some quite dark stuff—human sacrifice and the like."

As irrelevant as it now was, Frank was intrigued. "What is a thought-form?"

"Much what the name implies: Thought given physical form; a spirit manifested bodily through willpower alone."

A crazy thought struck Frank. "Could...?"

"Could what?" asked Henderson.

"No, I'm just being silly..."

"No, go ahead, old man."

"Well, I was just wondering. If one were to suppose such a thing could exist...could someone, uh, project an image of themselves—their consciousness."

"Yes. It has been claimed. The Theosophists speak of the astral body and say it can roam the spiritual dimensions. That could be made manifest. And, you will have heard of doppelgangers, of course."

"Uh-huh. And, could such a projection continue to exist after the death of the body?"

"Interesting that you would ask that... This fellow came to that conclusion, believing he could cheat death. Of course, he also believed he would need to commit repeated acts of murder to sustain it."

"Oh...Uh, thank you, very much."

"You're welcome, old man."

Frank felt a fool to be traipsing through the London backstreets in search of a dead man. He had always believed that dead meant dead and given little credence to ghosts, and yet now...Ridiculous! But, nonetheless, here he was, an evening fog coiling about his legs, like an over-affectionate cat, doing just that. It was like a scene from Dickens, rather than something from the 1920s. At times, he wondered what had happened to progress; had it died in the war?

There were few people about, but to those he met, he would proffer a photograph of McKintosh and enquire if they had seen him in the district. So far, the query had been met by a dozen shakes of the head.

An old man, in a worn-out great coat that might once have been army issue, shuffled towards him out of the shadows of the ill-lit street. As he drew nearer, Frank saw one sleeve hung limply by his side, devoid of an arm, another memento of the madness of the previous decade to remind them all to avoid a repetition of such folly in the future.

"Hello!" The man flinched at the sound of Frank's voice.

Frank held up his hands in what he hoped was a reassuring gesture. "I just wanted to ask if you've seen this man."

He held out the photograph and the man shuffled tentatively closer and looked at it. Frank waited as he examined the picture.

The old man nodded. "Yep, I seen him."

"Where?"

"Down there, the bookshop."

"Thank you." Frank reached into his pocket and produced a shilling, which he slipped into the man's hand, then strode off in the direction he had gestured to find the shop.

It didn't take long. The bookshop was in a dark side-alley. It was possessed of grimy windows, as if it were not intended to attract customers. Frank wondered if that were so, after rubbing some of the dirt from the glass and peering inside, for it appeared to sell occult books and accoutrements and was, perhaps, the sort of shop that acquired custom by word-of-mouth alone. No address was given, but he would have been willing to bet it matched that on the bill of sale.

He knocked on the door. There was no reply.

Somewhere, in the distance, a dog barked.

There appeared to be living quarters over the shop and Frank was certain McKintosh was within. He reached a decision and took out a tiny bag of tools: he would attempt to spring the lock.

A moment of jiggling wire later, there was a click and the door creaked open.

Frank returned the pouch to his pocket and stepped inside.

The interior of the shop was dark and as grimy as the exterior with dusty shelves stocked with old books with odd names, and unusual items, such as tiny cauldrons and oddly-shaped pieces of crystal.

There was a door behind the counter at the far end of the shop and, as he approached it, he became aware of a muffled sound reminiscent of the chanting of monks.

"Odd..."

Frank opened the door to reveal a short passageway ending at a door with one to either side. He tried the one to the left: it led into a storeroom full of boxes and crates. The one to the right concealed a staircase going up to the rooms above. The door at the end led to a cellar – up from which came the sound of chanting.

Frank drew his revolver, a trusty Webley and Scott. He didn't want to believe the theory that had brought him here, but, if it had any basis in fact, it cast the chant in a dubious light, especially given what Henderson had had to say about the man's beliefs.

Frank descended the steps, grateful that the sound rising up from the darkness covered that of the creaks his feet produced. He paused as he neared the bottom and looked into the room.

The cellar was square and lit by two braziers. A naked man holding a curved and ornately-decorated dagger stood at its centre. He looked uncannily like John McKintosh. At his feet was a second unclad man, trussed like a pig ready for the slaughter. Behind the tableau, at the far end of the room, stood a statue that represented some grotesque man-beast, clawed and fanged and red coloured, something that might have been torn from Hindu myth, but could equally have come from some medieval volume on demonology or straight from a nightmare; Frank was no expert, but he was certain it depicted evil.

It was McKintosh, Frank could no longer doubt it was him, who was chanting. Frank didn't recognise the words, save for what sounded like 'Hecate' and 'Strix', which he recalled from his schooldays.

He stepped forward, gun raised. "Stop!"

The man looked at him in surprise.

"John McKintosh, lay down your weapon."

"How—?" That confirmed it. Surprised, he lowered the blade, but, then, began to intone a series of guttural and broken syllables.

Frank suddenly felt as if his veins had filled with ice water. He shivered and groaned. He was growing colder. Weaker. The gun was so heavy. His arm began to sag.

Behind McKintosh, the statue seemed to shiver, as if it were waking from sleep. Claws twitched. Lips curled back.

"No!" Somehow, Frank managed to raise his revolver and fire, twice.

McKintosh stumbled backwards, dropping the dagger.

The chill seemed to vanish from Frank's veins and the statue was just that again.

Frank fired once more.

He blinked. McKintosh was gone. One moment, he was starting to topple, the next he had vanished. There was no blood, yet he knew three bullets had struck the man. Had he not seen it, he wouldn't have believed it, despite the thought that had drawn him here.

It took him a moment to recover. He glanced again at the statue, just to be sure. Then, he knelt down and cut the bound man free.

"Go, and tell no-one what happened here. If you can't

find your clothes, take some from the quarters above the shop."

The man nodded, mumbled his thanks, then stumbled to his feet and clambered unsteadily up the stairs and out of the cellar.

Frank looked around and shook his head, feeling bemused. His headache was returning.

He couldn't believe any of it, yet he couldn't doubt what he had seen.

>~⊂⊃ ⊂⊃~<

"I have Doctor Reed's report here, Mrs. McKintosh, confirming that it was your husband's body in the grave. And, I managed to trace the man in London, as well, and can say, without any reservation, that your husband is most-definitely dead."

Anne McKintosh dabbed her eyes with a handkerchief, then smiled at him. "Thank you, Mr Issland."

Frank felt satisfied that she was at peace, but the case continued to nag at him as he left the house. Just what had he experienced in that cellar? Was it real? Had he shot a man or a ghost? Doubt had begun to creep in upon him as soon as he had stepped back out into the cool night air, diluting his certainty, yet there was a core that would not be dismissed. He shivered.

Frank had left the task of dealing with the contents of the shop, and in particular, the unnerving statue, to Henderson. Although he suspected others may have been slaughtered in that cellar, he had decided not to contact the police, not knowing what to tell them. Now, he would do his best to put the events out of his mind.

He stopped in mid-stride. There was a figure standing in the shadow of the hedge, a little further down the lane. He was masked by darkness, and yet...

Frank ran across the lane, but there was nobody there.

"I must have imagined it," he murmured, trying to convince himself, all the while wondering if it were possible for McKintosh to have imagined himself a second thought-form. "Surely not..."

Frank shuddered. Then, he pulled the collar of his coat up against the evening chill and resumed his walk towards the train station, striding as quickly as he could, determined to leave it all behind him.

THE PINCH

M·A· SMITH

AN OLD CROOK once told me your average man on the street was becoming so suspicious that if you tried to lift his wallet you'd as soon get a mousetrap snap shut around your hand as score a fat wad of cash.

It didn't stop me wanting to try, though, and Charlie The Barley knew all the tricks. He was an old school grifter, and took great pride in imparting his trade to a humble apprentice, such as I was then. His area of expertise was agricultural theft, but he'd been a pickpocket since his childhood days and there was, to my knowledge, none better on the Jubilee Line. Seeing him at work among the pigeons as they barged and bolshed on and off the trains was some sort of poetry in motion. I couldn't get enough of it. And I was a fast learner. Time came that I was able to leave The Barley's tutelage and make a path for myself on the London streets.

I had a day job of course. Most of us do. You'd be surprised at how respectable we look. How much like you.

But I had plenty of opportunity to ply my trade on busy morning commutes, or after work, as queues gathered outside theatres and galleries, and pigeons of culture were eager to flash around their baubles.

I invested most of my earnings; there was a guy I knew through The Barley called Mickey, who 'converted' jewellery or what-have-you into cash, for a not unsubstantial cut. The deal with this was I had to get to him within two hours of the lift. Now, you could ask, quite reasonably, how this fellow would possibly be any the wiser if I turned up with the goods half an hour late, a week late, five minutes late. You move in my circles, though, you find out sharpish that these sort of folks do know. And if you doubt it, get coy about it, try to push your luck the one time, you may find that your life alters from that point on. Maybe you start suspecting that someone's shadowing your steps as you mosey down the Edgeware Road. You find your apartment door open one evening when you know you locked it that morning. Perhaps the next day you don't show up for your day job at all. And maybe the next week there's a new grifter working your patch. One that knows to get to The Barley's man within two hours of a lift.

A summer came when, though, I was considering calling time on the City. I'd put away nearly enough in ready money to begin thinking about taking up the sort of rural life that involves shotguns and trips to muddy floored, over heated pubs serving real ale and pork scratchings that still have bristly little hairs attached to their rinds.

I talked to my broker and calculated that one more season should do it, saving at the rate I had been. I'd maybe have to forego some of my more expensive...'tastes' for a month or so, but I thought I (and a number of Soho's more charming residents) could live with that. You could say I upped production, and as autumn blew in, skittering leaves along Tower Bridge like the dried and brittle bones of dead mice, I found myself staying on the streets later, and covering patches I hadn't worked for years.

A smoky dusk was lingering over the city the evening that I picked the pocket of the woman wearing the red hat, in a side street off Piccadilly Circus. She was looking at the menu stuck to the window of the restaurant she stood outside of. She wore a long black coat, and above its rounded collar slithered a red tattoo that coiled around her neck to disappear beneath her hat. Its inky scales pulsed with her breath, a sinuous and intimate movement that troubled me.

I sensed promise, though, so tugged my own hat a little lower, adjusted my scarf, and strolled slowly over to stand a few paces away from her, cupping my hands to the glass as I pretended to look into the restaurant.

After a few seconds I spun away from the window, feigning a sudden remembrance, mocked up a stumble, and collided gently with the woman. She instinctively moved both arms slightly up and out as her centre of gravity shifted, I put a hand on her arm to apologetically steady her, while my other hand slipped unnoticed into her coat pocket and lifted out what felt like a purse and a piece of jewellery. We both muttered quiet exclamations of apology, and parted. Done. Oldest trick in the book. I rounded the corner, without hurrying, and walked to the tube station.

I discreetly looked over what I'd hauled while I sat on the train, waiting for the Hammersmith stop to see Mickey about converting various bits and pieces from the evening's work. The red hatted woman's purse was a nondescript affair with perhaps a fiver in change inside. I'd maybe read the pigeon wrong: happens sometimes. What

I'd taken for jewellery turned out to be a strangely shaped coin. It was like no coin I'd seen before, though: made of steel or iron, it was three sided, with a pattern of spiralling numbers on one face and a Medusa type figure on the other. The figure's face was worn almost completely away. It weighed much less than it looked like it should.

I tucked the coin away and swung off the train as it slowed to a halt. Tugging on my gloves I noticed a fine reddish powder on my fingers. I stopped, and the human tide parted messily around me, surging into the street and dispersing into the London suburbs like dust. I pulled the coin back out, and saw what I'd missed before: that same red tinged powder clung to its three sides, impacted deep into the metal's tiny nicks and crevices.

It was full dark by then, and a bitter rain flickered in the cool orange glow of the sodium lights outside. I pushed the coin into my pocket, brushed my hands, hard, on my trousers, and hurried through the emptying streets to this grimy little lane between a newsagent's and an offy: not a place that shouted 'criminal underbelly of London.' Well, one wouldn't want to attract the wrong sort of notice.

I strolled into Mickey's 'office' feeling not quite as chipper as I maybe appeared. We conducted a number of transactions around items I had scored earlier that evening (although, you understand, well within the two hour window), and then I gave him the three sided coin, fully ready for disparagement and hoping I could at least winkle a few quid out of him to compensate for the tube fare. Instead of doing either or both of these things, though, The Barley's man slipped into a mysterious little back-room that I'd never been given the entry of. I could only make out the vaguest of murmurings as he conversed with an unknown associate on the phone. When he came out he was pale, and I noticed, with a not unsympathetic jolt, how old he'd grown during the years of our business acquaintance. He may have taken me for thousands in cuts, but he wasn't a bad chap. Calling him a lovable rogue would be like calling a medieval castle's dungeon a bijou apartment, but he wasn't the worst. By far.

Mickey lay a brick of notes on the desk between us. I made it disappear.

"Maybe best to move your business elsewhere, son," he said to me.

"Making you look bad, Mickey?" I returned, a growing unease coiling in my belly and winding a long tail up my gullet.

"That's right, sweetheart. Making me look bad. I hear Brighton's the place these days."

He produced a card from his sleeve. "Call this guy when you get there. Tell him my name."

With that, the old cudgeon retreated into the back office once more, leaving me bemused, but with the better part of two thousand nicker in my back pocket for that weird little coin with the Medusa on one side.

There being little else to do, I set off home to Northfields, still puzzling, and still with a slightly nauseating sense of disquiet. Opening the door to my apartment, I went straight to the bedroom and lay down fully dressed and shoed, my mind racing and my pulse not entirely steady. I was sure that sleep wouldn't pick the lock of my buzzing brain, but I soon found the light of my consciousness dimming to a fine point, until finally it was extinguished altogether, and I knew no more.

An old crook once told me, you only leave a job half done when either a copper's breathing down your neck or you get a better offer.

I wasn't getting any heat from the law, and I couldn't see a quicker way to reach my clichéd little cottage in the country but to carry on as was, so I decided to commit the whole incident with the coin to the nether regions of my memory and put Mickey's bizarre behaviour down to some sort of personal crisis. It was hard to do, though. Almost impossible. Especially when every morning I woke to find that same red dust on my fingers, no matter how many times I washed it off. Every single morning it covered my hands like pollen, leaving stains on my sheets and reddish rust around the basin when I sluiced it away...only for it to re-appear again the next day. I wore gloves to bed one night but discovered, on peeling them off at dawn, that same hateful powder on my skin, beneath the fabric. It was easiest to believe that I had developed an unusual skin disorder than consider the alternatives, and so that is what I did, even going so far as to procure a steroidal cream that I applied to my hands each morning, after removing the powder from my fingers. In this way, the top part of my brain, the more gullible part, convinced the wiser part underneath that everything was fine. That underneath part knew better, though. It always does.

The worst was to come. An awful, aching, *pinching*, sensation wracked my hands, so that sat in the sterile office where I spent my days, I could, at times, barely force my fingers to curl around a ringing telephone. I began to suspect arthritis, as I watched the joints stiffen and solidify, like little fossilizing corpses. Barely a week after the first presentation of these symptoms, I was working the pigeons pushing off the tube at Green Park, always a rich fishing ground as excited pigeons of the tourist variety were all glazed over with the thought of Buckingham Palace and all that old tosh. In hindsight, it was foolish, attempting a lift in the state I was, but there had taken root in my mind a kind of desperation, a weird feeling that perhaps if only I acted as though nothing had changed, miraculously, nothing would have.

It was a clumsy job, even without my mangled hands. The mark felt the jolt before my fingers even came into it and turned, all suspicion and hostility, looking at me with eyes that clocked my every feature. I only caught the clichéd 'What the...' as I melted back into and through the crowd. I sprinted on foot to the next tube station and caught the first train that came down the line. And what do you know, ended up back at Piccadilly Circus where this whole sorry palaver began. That my mind was far from clear is the only excuse I have for my footsteps taking me, as if following an unseen track from which there was no detaching, to the dark little side-street where I'd first encountered the woman in the red hat maybe a fortnight past. If I told you that she stood there still, right outside that closed up restaurant, as if she'd not moved since, you would quite rightly think that my mind had come loose under the pressure of my double existence, and maybe doubt the credibility of the whole of this tale. And maybe you'd be right; maybe I'm right now spinning my wheels in an institution somewhere, rattling on to an orderly about nicking wallets, women with weird tattoos, and an infinite red powder that covered the skin of my hands like an obscene dust.

Whatever the truth of it, I saw that woman standing there in the grey light, that fleshy snake tight to her neck and flashing now dull ochre, now silver to the beat of her pulse.

I came nearer.

My hands shook inside my pockets, and I felt the familiar ache intensify, so that it was like a foot stood on each, grinding the small bones beneath the skin and pulling, nauseatingly, at the tendons.

She turned her head to look at me, and I saw how the tattooed snake crossed her temple before sliding beneath the fabric of her hat. I can't explain this next part very clearly; the best I can do is to tell you that she began to talk to me, but her speech was in no language I have heard the like of before or since; guttural, and somehow meaty: animalistic. And that I was able to, in some horrific fashion, understand the sense of it. I realised, too, that, up close, I couldn't see her face clearly. It seemed to shift and swim and never come completely in focus, as if I were looking at her through spectacles with strong prescription lenses.

The essence of what she said was that old chestnut: "You have something of mine."

I held my hands out in a gesture I hoped would indicate that the coin was no longer in my possession. I also bought from my pocket, with withered fingers, a little pile of notes, and proffered it. "Please."

She touched my hands with hers, and the feeling of her skin on mine was so grotesque that I barely suppressed a scream.

Before turning away, she gave my fingers a last caress.

"Keep the change," she said.

SPIRIT IN THE SKY

MARLIN BRESSI

Lt. Benjamin Brooks took one final loving glimpse at his de Havilland DH-4 before softly closing the hangar door and retiring to his suite at the Roosevelt Hotel. Brooks, who served four unspectacular years in Britain's Royal Air Force, felt for the first time in his life that he was on the cusp of achieving something spectacular. In the morning he would be chasing the biggest prize in aviation; the Orteig Prize—a $25,000.00 paycheck for the first aviator to fly from New York to Paris.

It was a feat that had been unaccomplished since 1919, when New York millionaire Raymond Orteig first announced the prize. Lt. Brooks, however, felt that it was his destiny to become the first person to fly across the Atlantic. After all, aviation was in his blood; his father, Warren "Ace" Brooks, was a hero of sorts during the First World War, having pioneered the use of the zeppelin in bombing raids for the Royal Flying Corps. Even though his father met his demise at the hands of the dreaded German

Jagdgschwader over France, Lt. Brooks refused to give up flying. Unfortunately, the death of his father led Benjamin to be quite superstitious.

Benjamin's first attempt at the Orteig Prize was thwarted one year earlier in 1926, when a spiritualist sent him a letter pleading for him to reconsider his mission, stating that she had received a "warning from beyond." Lt. Brooks, after some deliberation, abandoned his chase of the prize. But he would not be thwarted this year, he kept telling himself.   Gypsies and fortunetellers be damned! Only the very voice of God could prevent him from climbing into his de Havilland DH-4 and setting sail across the sky.

Inside his suite at the Roosevelt, the silence of night was shattered by the ringing of a telephone. The weary aviator grumbled, knowing that it was probably just another well-wisher. Before Lt. Brooks had an opportunity to speak, an eerie disjointed voice moaned through the receiver. Benjamin thought it sounded like a man speaking into the whirling blades of an electric fan.

"Who is this?" demanded Lt. Brooks.

"It's your father," hissed the mysterious voice. "Ace."

"That's absurd!" replied Benjamin. His father had been dead since 1918. Suddenly aware that he had probably fallen into the snare of a prankster, he decided to ask the speaker from where he was calling.

"Somewhere just outside of heaven," replied the night caller.

Maybe that was just a lucky guess, thought Benjamin. But how would any American know about a deceased—and relatively obscure—WWI British airman?

"Ben, you must not fly tomorrow," pleaded the voice. "The sky will hurl you back to earth in a million fiery pieces."

The lieutenant was now almost certain that he had a prankster on the end of the line. Rather than hang up the night caller, however, he decided to ask a question that only an experienced aviator—or his father himself—would know the answer to. "If you are my father, then tell me what in the name of Wilbur Wright am I doing in an outdated war-era de Havilland. She's just a—"

"A two-seated bi-plane," interrupted the mysterious caller. "With a 380-horsepower Rolls-Royce engine. You chose the DH-4 because it was the same plane I had flown in the war. When you were a young lad, I would always tell you what a magnificent machine the DH-4 was."

"True. But the American version..."

"The American version of the DH-4 was built with a 400-horsepower Liberty L-12 engine."

"That's remarkable!" exclaimed Benjamin. "How? How could you possibly know that? The Americans didn't have their own DH-4 until..."

"Two months after I died," groaned the caller. "I told you that it was me, Benjamin."

"Why does your voice sound so strange?"

"It takes an enormous amount of energy to come back to the material plane," explained Ace. "Which is why so few of us are able to speak to the living. But it is possible for us to come back in order to give a warning to loved ones."

"Dad, what is heaven like?" asked the mystified young aviator.

"Remember the way you felt the first time your plane left the ground? Heaven feels like that, all of the time. Some people think flying is a way to play God, but the truth is that man flies in order to get closer to God." After a moment of silence, the gloomy voice added: "And anyone foolish enough to think that he can fly a war relic like the DH-4 across the Atlantic is bound to meet his Maker directly."

"Then why should I fear death?" asked Benjamin. "Why should I not fly tomorrow?"

"Benjamin," explained Ace, "A man should not fear death, but a man must not be in a rush to embrace it, either. Look, son, the Orteig Prize has never been claimed, so what harm will it do to wait one more day? Do you not hear the rain outside your window? Wait until Saturday, son, and the storm shall pass."

"As you wish, father," replied Benjamin.

The caller explained that since his work was done, he had to return to the spiritual realm. He wished his son well, and said that he was proud of him. Lt. Brooks returned the phone to its cradle and quickly drifted off to sleep.

Inside of a gray airplane hangar a few miles away, a cord was pulled from the wall socket and an electric fan's blades whirled to a stop. "You sonuvabitch!" laughed a man in a yellow raincoat. "I can't believe you pulled it off. He really is a superstitious fool, isn't he? With Brooks out of the way, that twenty-five grand is as good as in the bank."

"Your plane is finally ready to go," said a grease-stained mechanic, who pointed a wrench toward a sleek new monoplane with the name *Spirit of St. Louis* emblazoned on the nose. Mr. Lindbergh stood up, walked over to the hangar door and gazed upon the wakening dawn peeking over the horizon through the quickly dissipating morning drizzle. He could tell that it was going to be a wonderful day.

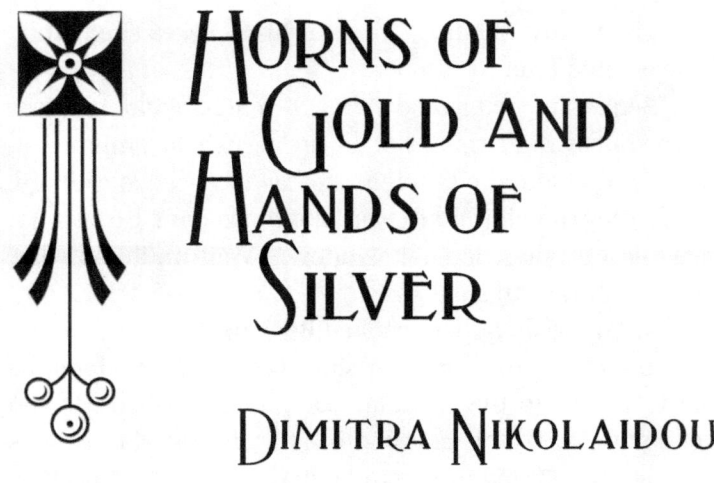

Horns of Gold and Hands of Silver

Dimitra Nikolaidou

The King of a Thousand Stories rolled into town when least expected.

But this time, we're prepared for him.

It's never easy, getting us Stolen Ones to work together. Yet rumors of the Fey King prowling the Grunewald, a forest so close to Berlin, will always unite us. None of us wants to go back to the King's Otherland. Not ever.

I first hear the rumors at the Zahngarten cabaret, while fixing the bronze beer dispenser for the third time this month. There is nothing really wrong with it, but the bartender, Bert Bearskin, has hands like claws. This is not a metaphor; those of us abducted by the Fey King as children sometimes escape his realm, but we always carry his stories on our bodies, which is why Bert is a menace to everything more delicate than a tractor. Thankfully, my own silver hands can reach where other tools can't; by the time Little Lady Lotte has finished her second song on stage, the dispenser is functional again. I turn to Bert to gloat, but he is looking past me, past the stage, a worried look on his broad face.

It only takes a glance to see what has him so worked up. The Zahngarten is always full of our kind, since few other places keep the drinks of the Otherland under the counter. Tonight, however, it looks as every single one of the Stolen is gathered here. And instead of partying or fighting as usual, everybody is huddling in the back tables, talking fervently, whispering, exchanging wooden coins for iron bullets.

I glance at the Sleeping Beauties: the humans, who can see neither our horns nor our stars. They are either looking at the stage, transfixed by Lotte's song, or laughing at each other's jokes, smoking and drinking, oblivious to the drama unfolding at the back. No, if something big is on tonight, it's coming for the Stolen alone.

"Bert? Do we know what's wrong?"

"They found antler horns in the Grunewald. Gilded ones."

Icy fingers melt down my spine. Gilded horns can only mean one thing: the Fey King is prowling the forest, either looking for more human children to steal or trying to recapture his escaped slaves – us. And for all the beauty of his face and the wonder of his realm, each and every one of us would rather die than go back.

Bert says nothing more, lets me catch my breath. I take the drink he pours for me without thanking him and head for the back, to join the rest of the Stolen.

"What can I do?" I find myself asking Ivar von Lindbergh. It could be his own antlers, which make me think he might know something more, or it could be the aura he projects. He was a hero in the Great War, and he still looks like the one you want to turn to in the middle of a crisis.

"There you are, Leira. Before you tell me anything, I need to know one thing from you and one thing only. Is the beer dispenser fixed?"

His voice is soft and musical. It could calm you even if you stood at the edge of the abyss, one foot in the air. I smile, despite myself.

"It is for tonight, Sir," I said. "Bert will break it again tomorrow, but until then all is well with the world."

"Hear that, people? Leira has already taken care of the most important part for us. Now let us deal with the easy stuff."

Everybody laughs; so do I. Even Max Vogel smiles at me and I gasp a little, for his smile is rare, and whenever I catch a glimpse of it, it always makes my week.

"Max, fill Leira in on our plans so far," says Ivar, bless his horns. "They were your idea, after all."

"What plan is that?" I ask Ivar, because I still cannot make myself talk to Max directly, but the General only smiles at me and leaves us for Lady Syphilis, who is distributing supplies from her bottomless medical bag.

Max takes time to light his cigarette. I don't mind. The light of the match makes him look like a graveyard angel. Part of me knows his charm comes from his Otherland days, for no normal beauty would be enough to distract me from the situation at hand, but that part has a really squeaky voice and I ignore it.

"Well, Leira," he says and the cigarette is dancing on his lips, muffling all his vowels, "my thinking goes something like that. We are in 1928. We do not live in wooden houses anymore, with only a rowan twig and a pinch of salt to ward off the creatures of the wood. Iron swords and enchanted shields are fine and well, but why not enchant a tank this time? Pit it against the King's horses and hounds, and see how tough he really is in our days of steel and petrol?"

Three thousand 'noes' rush to my lips, but no valid argument comes forward.

"A...a tank?" I ask. Max smiles, ear to ear. Against my better judgment, I smile back. "I suppose it could work," I say, and then remember his smiles are enchanted, his own Otherland gift. He is not even doing it on purpose, so I gather my wits. "Provided we find a tank. Are the Americans mailing us one? Because as far as I know, the Versailles Treaty still won't let us play with those."

"Well, Ivar and Erwin did not tell me 'no' outright, and they are our Generals."

I turn to look at them, the man with the deer antlers and the man with the dragon wings, whispering in the corner, not arguing for once.

"I should go talk to them then," I tell Max. He nods. I search for something to say before I go, come up empty, try again and then he gives me a cigarette. I stick it in my mouth, cup the flame he offers, watch the light dance on the engravings of my silver hands, smile, and finally, I leave.

I don't even smoke.

"Are we there yet?"

"No, Fraulein Allerleirauh," Erwin von Reinhardt says. He sounds amused, he always does. Ivar turns back and smiles at me. They could not decide who would drive the car, so they drew lots. Erwin won, so Ivar is now sitting beside him, judging his every move. All the while, all I can think of is the tank. I should have known the Versailles Treaty would not hold for long, but I hadn't realized it had been silently broken already, that some among us are already walking under the shadow of yet another war. But I shan't linger on the thought now, either. All that matters for the next two days is that we have in our possession something the Fey King has never faced before.

Well, also that I have a new type of machine to play with tonight. Since my escape, without a home to go back to but gifted with these enchanted hands, I survive by taking work where I can get it—trains, factories, repair shops. I can fix everything and I can do it quick. But tonight I will get a chance to toy with something really big, and the notion fills me with anticipation, even under the growing shadow of the Fey King.

Fraulein Kristel, sitting beside me in the back seat, does not share my enthusiasm. She sits beside me clutching her beaded bag full of enchanted gems, sighing under her breath, caressing the silk of her skirt with nails made of diamonds. She hasn't spoken a word since we explained our plan to her, save to ask us if we were ready to leave. Of all the things I should be afraid of—the Fey King, the tank that should not be, the improbability of our plan, Max Vogel's lips—somehow the petite jewel maker is the one who intimidates me the most tonight.

I don't like the taste of fear in my mouth, so I take a breath and speak.

"So, have you done this before?" She turns her bejeweled eyes to me, and she sighs, prettily as a breeze over water.

"I enchanted the reins of our horses the last time the King paid us an unsolicited visit," she says. "Does it count?"

I shrug. "Sure. It's not as if one thing makes more sense than the other. If our magic can work on steel swords, it should work on cannons too."

"Somehow, I cannot picture an enchanted tank in my mind," she says and I grab my chance.

"Why not?" I say. "The Fey King beats us every time because he forces us to take part in his stories, right? But if we stand against him in a modern tank, if we use something he hasn't seen before, then we force him into one of our stories instead. It is the only way we can have a fighting chance."

Her distant gaze makes me speak much more and much faster than I would otherwise, but I am surprised to find that my words make sense, and as I speak them, belief in the project is forged stronger inside my chest. Then Erwin hits the brakes outside what seems to be the middle of the forest, and I realize we have arrived.

I get out and gather my leather coat around me. Ivar picks up my bag of tools for me. No point in telling him I can lift a car if need be; it is the principle of the thing. As they secure the car, I bargain with the forest. We were all taken as children near a place such as this. We had all walked through the familiar woods into a place where all our dreams had come true in the worst possible way. I stare at the tiny stars, chased up the sky by the black tips of the trees, and wonder if I would ever make peace with the quiet night again.

"Leira?" Ivar says. I turn and follow him. As the four of us walk the forest path, the trees thicken and multiply, growing closer and closer to each other, until their trunks melt into walls of wood. Then, the walls of wood smooth into walls of gray cement. And just like that, we walk into a warehouse filled with metal shapes glinting into the scant moonlight, everywhere the scent of diesel and welding and warm metal.

Erwin von Reinhardt turns on the light, and I draw the sharpest breath. Tanks in every stage of assembly are all around us, sheets of metal and boxes of screws lie half-opened, huge blueprints hang on the walls. I turn my head, then stop, holding back, then spin around on the spot to take it all in. These are not the clunky tanks of the Great War. These are new.

"Where are we?" Kristel asks. The Generals had guided us through a fairy path; we could be anywhere in Berlin.

"We cannot tell you," Ivar says. "The location is a state secret; I am sure you can appreciate the reasons. This is why none of you will enter or exit the warehouse through the door. However, we can stay and work all night if need be. Just tell us what to do, Leira, and we will do it."

"I need to see the blueprints first," I say, already standing in front of a huge, wooden board, trying to make sense of the design pinned upon it. I had never seen a tank in action of course. I was taken before the Great War; escaped after it had finished. I would hear the men talking about them sometimes, telling me why it was impossible to lose with such beasts on our side, complaining it was the politicians who stabbed our army in the back. I never gave such words much thought, thinking we were just comforting ourselves about our loss, but now, standing among the sea of metal, I could at least understand why they felt this way.

I could understand why Max had suggested we fight the Fey King with a tank.

＞—ᗞ   ᗞ—＜

"I'm almost done," Kristel says. "Just let me add a few more rubies to the fire."

I look at her pushing her last glowing gem down the barrel; I feel the magic flow from her fingers into the steel. Inside me, a different fire burns. The fire that the Fey King had kindled inside me, to allow me to construct so many wonders for him in his enchanted realm. The gift had cost me my hands. Tomorrow night, it would cost him his life.

At least, I hope it will.

I circle my masterpiece slowly. We had to use the warehouse discards, of course, but this was never a problem for me. I work better with scraps, with bits, with what others leave behind. Kristel is different of course; she is an artist of the enchanted and the mundane, and not a mechanic. It was she who had insisted on the bronze dragonfly in the front, the vertical lines, the bronze sheen.

We are going to wage war in an art deco statement piece.

I don't mind. I love it. It is much lighter than an actual tank, since we won't be going against any kind of firearms, and it's enchanted from the cupola to the caterpillars. I had personally turned every last one of the screws with my hands, placed plates of iron under the panels' steel, I had calibrated the cannon thrice. It will work. It has to work. Or we will all dance in the Fey King's tunes for eternity, and this is out of the question.

"So, did you think to make me a velvet seat? With plump armrests and a little footrest for me to extend my legs?"

Max Vogel is still smiling but I am too exhausted to stutter this time.

"You mean you will be driving the tank?"

"I told the Generals I should do it. I did it in the Great War, I haven't forgotten a second of these days."

"Well, I hope your butt remembers too, because the seat is tiny. But if it's any consolation, Kristel has sculpted a pretty dragonfly on the outside."

"Does it do anything?"

We are sitting in the Zahngarten, only it's morning now and it's empty. I have taken three whole chairs for myself, and I am looking up the ceiling. It's full of last night's glitter, slowly dislodging itself and descending upon our heads like a poor man's falling stars.

I am glad I'm not working as a cleaning lady anymore.

"The eyes are sapphires. They will lull the King's dogs into a deep sleep."

"Anything else I should know?"

"I'm sure the Generals will tell you everything. Once they get over the fact that their tank looks like a party piece," I say.

"You are angry."

"They were a bit too proud of their warehouse. One look at the blueprints, and I could already tell what kind of havoc these machines can wreak. I don't want to survive tonight only to find myself into yet another Great War tomorrow."

"I prayed for peace in the trenches, when I was just a kid. It was the Fey King who answered," he says and I shudder. I open my mouth to answer but he gets up and his face is now hidden in the Zahngarten's darkness.

"I'm sorry."

"Nah, don't be. Go to sleep. Tomorrow, everything will be beautiful again, Leira. You'll see."

Max Vogel had better be right.

He'd better be right about when he predicted the ancient Fey King would be no match for our mechanized armaments, and he'd better be right that tomorrow is going to be beautiful—because the night of the hunt has teeth, and smells of blood and fear.

Herr Weller, our scout, has been tracing the Fey King's tracks all day. Our former master is a creature of whim but his hunts are bound, by ancient habit or by unfathomable pacts with the forest itself, to a predictable pattern. They always last three days and three nights; his hounds and his horses run endlessly in concentric circles, their trajectory getting bigger and bigger until, on the third night, the forest delivers his prey: either a human child, or a former slave, someone who thinks themselves free until they are not.

And the Generals camouflaged the tank right in the middle of his path, hoping that the King's instincts would be no match for his momentum.

I shift in my seat in front of the machine gun, try to fit, and fail. I cross my legs, uncross them, attempt to sit on my hands. I breathe in, as silently as I can.

Waiting isn't my strong suit.

"Fix that for me?"

Erwin hands me his binoculars. He ended up the commander of the tank, when it became obvious that Ivar's horns didn't fit in the cupola. Now he stands, wings painfully folded back against the recoil pad, waiting to give the signal. Kristel, dressed in a military uniform that no doubt belonged to some hapless lover, is by necessity, the ammunition loader. Herr Korbes, yet another Great War veteran, has taken the gunner's seat. In a space so tight, I can almost feel the heaviness weighing down their limbs. Only Max Vogel radiates calm—I can sense his smile even though I only see the back of his head.

I take a single look at the binoculars and I immediately know that Erwin has unscrewed them just minutes ago, to give me something to do with my hands. Still, I get to it and it helps. Helps until the moment I hear scout Weller's voice coming into the radio, just a single word, a growl that floods my insides with adrenaline.

"The Hunt."

My body clenches and my stomach falls but I take my position right away, hands on the machine gun's grips, legs lost under me, breath hovering in my throat. I try to hear the hounds and fail; I get ready nonetheless and I wait for Erwin's command and when it comes and Herr Korbe moves to obey, I brace for impact as the pit in my stomach turns to an eruption of unexpected joy.

The cold iron missile, enchanted with Kristel's fire, should be wreaking a path through the Hunt. I cannot see it, but the entire cabin shakes and my body shakes along with it, and for a moment I am outside the cramped space, soaring above the tips of the trees, screaming my war cry.

And then the sounds come. The sounds of disaster, clumsily disguised as a rustling from the outside. It takes one look at Erwin's white face, to know that something has gone awfully wrong.

"Leira, fire the machine gun!"

No. No, no, no. But my hands obey, heavy as they have become, and I reach for the handle.

Nothing works.

I open my mouth to ask what is going on but then the light comes, unbearable starlight, slipping in as our tank opens up like a lotus flower. I turn and Erwin is already turning into a dragon, huge wings unfurling, limbs turning black, hands extending into claws. I see Kristel and Korbes lose their human shapes, twisting upon themselves too, turning into the fairy tales they thought they had escaped from. And then I turn to Max, and he is still human-shaped, and he is still smiling.

My heart skips a beat.

Now my creation is lying open around us, useless plates covered in bronze, gems empty of their fire lying on the grass of the night forest. And all around us the Hunt, panting, howling, pouring into their ever-turning circles.

Only these aren't the hounds I remember. These are made of brass and bronze, their eyes are agate and their joints are mechanical, leaking oil of gold, exhaling diesel fumes between their steely teeth. There is no way the sleeping charms would have worked on these things; I am lost. Yet they aren't coming for me; they are dispersing in the woods, where the rest of the Stolen are hiding in waiting, as if they know where to go. We aren't prepared for such a battle; it will be a massacre.

But why did they ignore me and run straight for the others? Someone is giving them orders, guiding their wrath away from me. I look left and right and I see nothing, no huntsman standing on the forest path, no King between the trees. And then, shivers spread from the top of my head down to my toenails. Slowly I look up and there it is, gliding over the treetops: a bird of thunder, made of dreamstuff and metal. A fusion of beast and steel that shouldn't be airborne, yet it is. And on its back, behind a glass cupola, a silhouette I know all too well. The shape of my King, dark and distorted behind the glass yet unmistakable. He is here; he has come for me. The dread that washes over me takes every thought away till in the end, only relief is left: It's over. I don't have to run anymore; there's nowhere to run to. All I have to do, is kneel and wait.

And then I hear a faraway scream and a metallic bark and I snap out of it, with only seconds to spare, for if he lands it will be too late. I grab Erwin's pistol from the ground, lift it and aim directly for the glass. I don't care if the King rides a Pegasus or this hybrid airplane, iron will always work on him.

"No!"

Max grabs my waist, shoves his weight on me and pins

me down on the ground. I scream from the bottom of betrayal and try to bite his hand but he's quicker; just like that, he unscrews my right hand and the gun rolls away from the limp fingers.

I can sense the King's smile in my bones.

"Why?"

"Why?" growls Max, going for my other hand even as I fight. "Because to hell with Berlin, that's why. Let him have us. Let him take us back where the wars are stories and hunger has a purpose. Let him take us back where there is at least some beauty in our damned suffering."

"Idiot!" I let him grab my other hand; his fingers search for the joint. This time, I turn the entire silver contraption around on the wrist, grab his fingers and bend them backwards until I break them.

He screams, lets go of me and rolls sideways. I ignore him. The King is driving his weird plane towards me and without thinking, I use my single remaining hand to pick up the hatch of our broken tank, and hold it high. The gems are drained of enchantment but the iron inside works and the King swerves abruptly enough to bend the trees.

Planes, even enchanted ones, never maneuver as well as a Pegasus would.

I search for the tank's tracks and run along them, as fast as the weight of the hatch allows me. They stop a few meters away and I know the fairy path we came through has to be there still. The plane is turning back and this time the King will be prepared; I drop my makeshift shield and dive between two tree trunks. I scramble and I run and just like that, I land among the tanks in the secret warehouse.

I don't turn on the lights. I climb inside a tank, pull down the hatch and curl upon myself. This late, I am alone. I can hear the guards talk outside, and share cigarettes with each other. I can hear their dogs barking. I can hear crying—mine.

It takes me some time to breathe again through the snot and the tears and the ball of lead in my chest. Some fairy tale heroine I turned out to be. Not noticing Max's sabotage on time, not moving fast enough to repair the damage, running away in the forest, leaving everyone behind, even losing a hand—again. And now I'm here, probably the last Stolen One in Berlin, crying my heart out inside a cold, steel pit. A fitting ending for the Fey King's dire tales. A fine warning to those who disobey him.

I wipe my nose on my sleeve—plenty of fabric flapping around now that I'm missing a hand—and climb out of the hatch.

And who is there but Max Vogel, sitting on the workman's bench, clutching my lost silver limb in his good hand.

"Please," he says. He doesn't sound in better shape than me. Not at all. "I just want to talk to you."

Anger devours all my words, leaving only short, heaving breaths behind. Max sees an opening, and takes it.

"I had to go back to him, Leira. Berlin has been eating me alive since I returned from the Otherland. The hunger, the fear, the dead-ends. I've walked the forest every night for years, hoping to chance upon his Hunt. I called him in my dreams. I ate glass and nails, just like in the stories, hoping to catch his eye once more. And one night, he left a message for me, pinned on a gilded antler on my bed. He would have me back, but only if I gave him a gift worthy of the pain I caused him by escaping."

"And you gave him us." The guards—I mustn't shout. I must keep it low.

He doesn't answer. He raises my severed hand up high, swallows his first words and takes a breath. "He has a deal for you now. If you will have it."

"I will end him."

"Please, Leira. He said he will let everyone go, if only you go to him willingly. And he will not bother Berlin again, for a year and a day."

"And you? What will you get out of it?"

"I will finally have delivered a gift worthy of my betrayal. And so, I get to follow you inside. Once there, I don't care what story he weaves out of me, as long as I have left Berlin. They are brewing another Great War, Leira, and I cannot go through the horror again; I would rather be shoveling fey manure in his stables than stay here to watch it happen all over again. But you, you will be his pride. You will make the stuff of dreams for him. You won't have to use scraps and discards anymore, like you do here—you will create all those modern wonders he cannot fathom and you will be his most enticing story." He pauses. "And back in Berlin, every Stolen One will be safe, thanks to you."

The cruelty of the Fey King, is like a feather net. It falls upon you slowly and you don't realize you are trapped until it's too late.

I look at Max. I want to ask so much, say so much, but in the end, I just extend my silver fingers. He seems to understand, and passes me my right hand.

"Will you do it? Will you deliver us all?"

I nod. "Not much choice, Max. It was my fault I didn't catch your act of sabotage, wasn't it? Ivar and Erwin trusted in me. I have to set this right."

"Thank you."

"But let him know, they must all be returned exactly as they were, before I follow him back. Every last one of them. And he has to promise me, that all I will be doing for him this time, will be to build stuff. No more stupid princes. No devils. No romances. No evil fathers. Just me in my workshop, doing my thing."

He keeps nodding. His eyes are red, and he doesn't dare smile.

"And tell him, I get to decide your story."

Even that doesn't dissuade him. I put my hand back in the stump, and try to move the fingers. It is damaged, almost broken, but with a bit of work I can make it whole again.

There is no Hunt for me this time. There isn't even a proper forest. The Fey King is evolving with the rest of us, it seems, and Max has arranged for me to return to Otherland in a mundane train carriage. I take the train at the Anhalter Bahnhof; I will exit in another world. If the King keeps his promise, and he always does, the Stolen Ones will already be on the train running parallel to mine yet going on the opposite direction—returning to Berlin.

The thought sustains me.

I sit by the window, look outside. I pay no attention to Max who walks in and sits opposite me. His steps are light, exuberant; he has taken nothing with him, not a suitcase, not even a memento. His broken fingers are healed already. The Otherland takes care of its children, after all.

He doesn't dare talk to me. What is there to say? When we leave the station, I stick my face closer to the window to take in my last fragments of Berlin, and he sighs relief under his breath.

The ride doesn't take long. Soon, I cannot feel the pistons under my seat. The smell of metal and coal subsides. I turn my face from the trees outside the window back to the wagon and there is no Max, only a crow flying away from his seat. I get up, and get out.

There is no enchanted forest waiting for me.

Instead, I'm in the middle of a train station, similar to the one I left behind. I look up to see a glass dome, supported by gilded girders. Planted in the walls, they erupt in golden flowers cascading to the marble floor. There are six different train tracks, completely empty save my single carriage. In a gilded booth, a uniformed bear is selling tickets. A tree is planted in the middle of the station, and newspapers hang from its branches like fruit. Winged vendors are selling delicious-looking food. It smells so much better than the crap I could afford in Berlin, and for a moment I want to go to them and beg for a bite.

Oh, I'm back all right.

The sound of hooves makes me turn my head, but instead of the gigantic deer I was expecting, I see an impossibly long convertible the color of olive leaves, sliding into the station. A bronze deer ornaments the hood; the wheels turn like a tide of gold. Yet for all its splendour, my eyes stay on the driver. He stops the car and gets out and I kneel out of habit, as if my legs were made to do just that.

How did I ever manage to escape? To see him is to surrender your will. He strides towards me in a coat made of white leather, a pilot's hood with matching goggles on his head, his boots crossing the distance as if it was nothing. And his eyes, blue like Kristel's dragonflies, smile at me despite my treachery.

"My King."

"You are back, Allerleirauh. I am so glad." Inside me, happiness combusts, bright enough to match his. "Have you learned all that you could, outside? Are you ready to return?"

"Learned?"

"The new world, that is out there. The machines, the engines, this new, sharp art. Have you absorbed everything there was? Are you ready for us to build new wonders together?"

I lift my head a little higher. He is taller than he was before, as if his true form can't be completely contained in the illusion of a man.

"You—you sent me outside so I could learn? I didn't escape on my own?"

He waves my concern away. "I had to. I am sorry you had to tolerate the streets of Berlin for so long, dear daughter, but even Otherland has to change with the times and I can't do everything alone. And children don't know machines, do they? No machine I snatched from their dreams works well, as you no doubt noticed at the forest. No, I had to send one of you away, and retrieve you later on. But forget about that. The terrors of the outside are gone. Tell me everything, Leira. Tell me of all the new things we are going to built together. Tell me how we are going to change the dreams of men."

Above us, the crow that was Max Vogel circles over the Fey King's head. There is nothing human in his flight, no sign of the suffering man who sold us for a pinch of fairy dust. I look at him and remember, how the flame of his lighter danced upon my silver hands.

"Buy a girl a drink first, my King?"

He smiles and extends his gloved hand. There is a grace in his fingers I now realize I had been looking for in every line I drew, every man I kissed behind the Zahngarten cabaret. I extend my own hands to touch them.

And then my silver hand unclips from the wrist, hanging only from a slim steel hinge, I point the stump towards him and I unload all my iron bullets in his chest.

His eyes widen and become lakes; his hands go to the hole in his chest, where the iron has broken the dreamstuff of his body in a thousand pieces. My own body screams with pain. I had to sacrifice my forearm for this and working with metal in a hurry is never a good idea, not to mention turning half your arm into a Gatling gun, but the pain on his face makes it all worth it.

For a few seconds anyway, because now his body is turning into shadow and the station begins to collapse around me, raining broken glass and golden shards upon my unprotected head.

I scramble and run to the convertible; he twists upon himself and his fingers extend like the roots of an ancient tree. I jump in, clasp my right hand back by slamming it on the wheel, and press the pedal. The car obeys, swerves on the platform, and I step on it. The glass plates on the station's door show me that he follows, a shadow creature riddled with holes; I lower my head and drive through them. Once I am out, full of cuts and broken glass, I turn around, unclasp my other hand and serve him his second portion of the meal. He retreats inside the crumbling station, and I hear Max Vogel's near human cry; I risk a backwards glance and there he is, my former friend, sitting on the now-empty cowl and mourning in a way that would shred my heart into pieces if the damned thing wasn't beating in my throat right now.

"Come with me," I scream to him "Max! Let's go back together". He doesn't hear, and even if he could hear me, he is too far gone. The fey station's façade fills with spidery cracks that branch and spread fast, criss-crossing each other again and again till the whole thing is nothing but tiny glass fragments suspended on the air. For an impossible second it remains standing and then, with a hollow sound, it crumbles into fine, glittery dust. I try to spot Max in the cloud but the wind starts blowing the powder my way, and I know I have to turn my back, step on the pedal, grab the wheel as if it was a life ring, and speed away.

They say to kill the Fey King inside his realm is to claim his power; they say he will be reborn in seven years' time. I won't stay to find out. I will drive all the way back to Berlin and when my car turns to leaves and nails, I will walk. I will walk through the forest and into the yellow lit streets of the city, where the food is scarce and what you see is what you get. And I will find my friends, who right now, are probably drinking in honour of my sacrifice, and I will laugh in their faces for thinking that nobody escapes the Otherland twice.

After all, I tell myself as I drive the beast back into Berlin, this is the age of wonders.

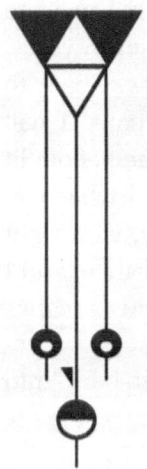

Two Steps Forward

Holly Schofield

I EASED MYSELF DOWN off the running board of the '28 Hudson sedan then laid a hand on the hood in mute sympathy for its overheated pistons. A quick buttoning-up of my topcoat and a tug on my fedora and I felt ready to approach the farmhouse.

The old woman on the veranda watched me as I drew close. Fly-away gray hair surrounded a narrow, clever face, faded housedress atop rubber boots, she was as much of a hodgepodge as I used to be. The late model Stewart Warner radio perched on the windowsill shimmied with *The Spell of the Blues.* I hummed along as the saxophones swooped and soared.

The old woman fingered the jumble of items on her lap as if looking for a weapon and I stopped a few feet from the bottom step of the porch.

"Afternoon, ma'am." I tipped my hat, not too far, and put my hands in my pockets. "I won't take up much of your time. Your husband built that famous automated scarecrow, am I right?" At her tightening mouth, I quickly added, "I'm not a reporter, just an admirer. I saw that scarecrow ace the dance marathon at the Playland Pavilion in Montreal last winter. Truly hep to the jive." The ballroom's mirrored walls reflecting the graceful moves of the dark-suited figure, hands as clever as Frisco twirling a chiffon-clad partner—a sight worth seeing, all right. The old woman grunted and picked up a dirty rag. She poured something golden and syrupy over it from a pickle jar, and began rubbing a coaster-sized metal disc—a flywheel? a gear?—with more vigor than necessary.

The sun beat down on my hat and heavy coat. Manitoba in August could cook a person's innards. Common courtesy would be to invite me onto the porch. She said nothing. I did as she'd expect and walked over to the shade of the big maple that crowded against the railing.

When she finally spoke, her voice grated like sand in a pocketwatch. "Yup, he built that thing." The words hung on the dust-filled air. She put down the disc and squinted into the shade where I stood. "He's dead and gone. I think you mebbe know that."

She'd lied with ease. Getting her to do what I needed would be harder than mastering the Lindy Hop.

"I heard that, ma'am, and you have my sympathies," I said, continuing to play innocent. "Can I ask, why didn't he build more than the one?" It had bothered me for ages and I'd thought about it the whole six-hour drive out here from Winnipeg. Why not make another of the marvelous two-stepping scarecrows? Dozens? Hundreds? The floorboards of the dance halls from here to Toronto could quiver from the beat of a thousand metallic toes.

"Why should I tell you about Abe's affairs? You a tax man?"

"No, ma'am. I'm not from the tax office." Not even

close.

"The bank, then. I s'pose you're here to hand me a late mortgage notice? I already got two."

"No, ma'am. I'm not from the bank. Just interested, is all. Music is my life."

"Well, even if you were foreclosing, there's nothing here you want anyway. No one will buy this land no more. With Abe gone, I can't put in a wheat crop and I sold off all the cows. No equipment worth a red cent, neither. Don't go thinking there's a fancy workshop here. That mechanical boy was constructed from cast-off junk: washing machine parts, broken wooden pipes, ball joints from the old John Deere's drive shaft. Junk, all junk." She paused and spat over the side of the railing. "Damn thing never did a decent stroke of work keeping the birds off my vegetables."

"With respect, ma'am, I heard the mechanical man was the cat's whiskers at hoofing around the joint, giving those wingèd pests the bum's rush."

My poetical words must have painted a fine picture—her shoulders relaxed slightly, like a dance marathoner on the second day. She finished polishing the gear and laid it on the old wicker table beside her, next to a tin can heaped with ball bearings. She picked up a smaller gear from her lap, with cogs the size of babies' teeth, and turned it over and over. "The head, doncha know, was an old tea kettle. The handle was busted so it got soldered back onto the side—made the funniest-looking ear you ever saw." The side of her mouth quirked up.

From my place in the shadows, I nodded several times. "The copper sheen made him look like he perspired when he danced." A certain swanky Winnipeg dance hall lit up my memory, the figures whirling in bright dresses and suits, foxtrotting to *Brother, Can You Spare a Dime*. The orchestra had so enchanted me that, at times, I had been oblivious to the torture of that twenty-six day marathon: the cruel catcalls from the paying audience, the MC's brutal "sprint" contests, the total exhaustion of my partner as she slept standing upright against my rigidly-held shoulder through the nights. Like all my partners, she kept her energy for dancing, not talking, so I never learned much about her beyond her name.

"He covered his head up, pretty quick, I heard tell, when he bummed his way east outta here. Got it coated with that newfangled Bakelite. Nobody could tell he wasn't a person, except for the steam coming out his nose spout." She peered over at me. "How'd you know his head was copper?"

Jeez Louise, call me a chowderhead! She might be near-sighted but she wasn't dim. I changed the subject fast. "One of the gossip rags said he got the nose fixed too, just redirected the steam to vent out several places on his body. The girls found him plenty steamy, all right. A real 'Lothario from Ontario.'" I laughed and was relieved to see the corner of her mouth twitch up further.

"Heard he won all the marathon contests from here to Montreal," she said, gruffly, leaning back enough to make the wicker creak. "Guess nobody else *could* make another one, or they would have—just to get the prize money."

Like a roadhouse gambler closing in on his patsy, it was time to show a little of my hand. If we didn't come to an understanding, all this was for naught.

"Nobody has your skill, ma'am." I let that sentence lie there, overlaying the chirp of the grasshoppers and the waltz that now drifted out the window, and took a big gulp from my hip flask.

The old woman cackled. "Smart as a whippersnapper, aren't you? Yeah, I built the damn thing. Kept me busy the winter before Abe passed, just like my new radio. Didn't want to admit to it, after the reporters started coming around. I started off real simple. I only wanted to keep the sparrows off my strawberries and such. Then he began dancing, slick as oil. Twirling around in the moonlight, all graceful and smooth, in that wrinkled-up swallowtail coat the undertaker gave me. After a few months, I stuck an old axle kingpin in his ankles so he could bend in all the right places. Never got a thank you." She leaned back and put her hands behind her. I couldn't quite read her expression.

I pictured the scene as a crow might see it: the scarecrow high stepping under the moon, tails flapping, twisting like the hepcat he would become. NBC's *Palmolive Hour* alive with sweet jazz, the hopeful scent of ripening tomatoes, and the moonlight playing among the carrot fronds. The scarecrow tap dancing madly to *California, Here I Come* as it blared out the window of the farmhouse he was never, ever invited into.

She leaned forward, studying me. "Nice coat," she said. I straightened the collar, pleased she had noticed. Camel-hair, with leather-covered buttons, it had been the feature in the Eaton's window all spring and had cost me the moola from my last three marathons. She spun a gear on her finger, round and round. "Bet it's hard to keep the coal dust off it."

We understood each other all right. I touched my chest with my gloved hands then held them out to her, in mute recognition of her statement.

Her voice rasped. "That mechanical boy never appreciated the oil I rubbed in his joints, the coal I shovelled beneath his boiler, the spot-welding when he broke a toe. He just up and run off, right before harvest. The birds poked holes in most of the squash before the sun had set that day. By golly, I should have made one leg shorter so he could only walk in circles."

"Perhaps," I said, "the radio is to blame."

"The radio?" She dropped the gear with a clank. "Well, I never! The radio!"

"Like peeking through a keyhole day after day, never being able to open the door. He wanted to see everything for himself, touch everything, live everything. You name it, he wanted it. Jam sessions, mellow rhythms, swell fellows and grooving chicks. He wanted it all."

"Horsefeathers!"

I jammed my hands in my pockets. Johnny Green's *Easy Come, Easy Go* finished its chorus and slid into a long bridge, silky as cream.

The old woman swayed a bit to the beat then caught herself. She must have cut quite a rug in her younger days. "A bum, a wastrel, that's what he is," she said, as if she'd said it many times before.

The wailing horns were drawing me in. I clenched my fists harder and tightened my knee joints, fighting the urge. I had to make her see. "Perhaps he wanted to do more than chase birds away, as if he was a deuce of tin pie plates banging in the wind. Perhaps he wanted to earn you some lettuce when Abe was huddled in bed with scarlet fever. But perhaps,"—I faltered then continued—"you'd rather let the bank seize the farm than take help from me."

Bridges burned, I stepped out into the sunlight, swept off my fedora, and let the sun beat down on my beige Bakelite-covered head. I opened my coat and took out the prize money from Toronto's Nationwide Super Marathon, laying the thick wad of cash on the top step of the porch.

The old woman stood up, heedless of the gears, springs, and other clockworks tumbling from her lap. She took the two steps necessary to grab the money and turned away, rubbing her eyes. Her gnarled hand wrenched open the screen door and she disappeared into the dimness beyond. The door slammed behind her so loudly the starlings took off from the clothesline in indignation.

I took another swig from my flask, the last of the kerosene failing to ease the tightness in my throat. Steam from several of my apertures drifted faintly up toward the gutters. A thank you would have been too much but I'd hoped for a friendly smile or a hi de ho. And a cup of her special lubricating blend would have hit the spot before I drove my car down the dirt track back to the highway, back to the dance halls, back to the bleak faces of the marathoners. I'd learned that dance floors didn't sparkle so much after the glitter dust got trampled. I was a scarecrow with a lot of dashed hopes, an excellent sense of rhythm, and a chest that was as hollow as a certain famous tinman.

My hand had cranked open the Hudson's door handle when the old woman hailed me, something bright in her hand. The crows mocked from the maple as I returned to the veranda, my new wingtip shoes causing aches in places I didn't know I had.

"Take the damn key ring," she said. "Go out to the smaller barn next to the coal shed." She waved a hand, impatient at my slowness in mounting the steps. "You need to wind them counterclockwise, light the kerosene-soaked coal, squirt all their joints with a drop or two of lubricant, and then explain to them about...well, about everything."

The keys jangled from my glove-clad fingers. "Them?"

"The other scarecrows. There's six ready in the barn and half a one in the workshop that's not finished yet. It's been a slow summer." She trudged back into the house, lifting her heels very slightly in time to *Sweet Sue, Just You.*

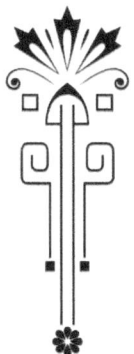

CHILDREN OF THE COIL

SEBASTIEN MANTLE

IT ALWAYS STARTS OUT the same, with the light. Through a haze I look ahead, to a luminescent wall that sears my retinas. And I feel a cold beyond the clammy chill of my soaked coat. The cold it has something to do with the slender speck of shadow at the base of the wall of light, growing and shrinking with the pulsations of swirling brightness. I cry out with a hoarse voice for the shadow to stop, to get away from the light.

It turns around, and for an instant I can see the glazed eyes of a young, gaunt-faced girl. She's smiling at me, and that smile freezes my blood. I reach out, but I know it's too late. She's too far away. The girl turns her brilliant smile towards the light, reaches to touch it...

I wake with a strangled shout, my chest tight. Sitting up, I clutch my sweat-drenched forehead, trying not to think about the dream. The memory. Avoidance, it's a morning ritual these days.

Beams of sunlight filter through my knockoff bamboo curtains. Eventually, the cold sweat dissipates, and I get up. I head to bathroom. After a shower, I pour a tumbler of bourbon from a bottle on the kitchen counter. The cheap stuff. When you choke down as much as I do, you stop caring about the taste. Wailing sirens and whistles of steam engines mingle outside into a cacophony of sound. I down my drink, pour another, and go to my window. A zeppelin casts its shadow from several meters overhead as it glides lazily through the sky above the sprawling city. I watch it drift through sinuous clouds of steam and smoke rising from the streets.

Below, sunlight gleams off the speeding monorail on its zigzagging way through this jungle of concrete and glass, taking commuters high above the ground to zip along between skyscrapers, trailing white steam behind it. This city is a sight to behold, but one thing inevitably draws my eyes beyond all else. In the center of it all stands the Coil. A spiraling tube of pulsating light trapped within a fortified glass and copper encasement, rising so far above the skyline its tip touches the clouds. They call it the future, a device that can wirelessly transfer infinite amounts of energy, anywhere. Free and limitless electricity. A huge glowing super conductor, right in the middle of one of the most densely crowded cities in the world.

I lift my glass to my mouth and drain it, letting burning alcohol sooth away some of the tension knotting my stomach. I go to the door, unlatch it, and blindly grab the rolled-up newspaper I know is waiting for me. Taking it to my armchair, a battered old thing upholstered in black leather in a dark corner of the room, I throw myself onto the worn cushion. I click on my lamp, cordless like all CoilTech technology, and flip through the paper. It's the usual Manhattan garbage. Political scandals, proposals for civic planning in the inner city, the closing of a famous pancake diner.

I almost flip past it, but one article catches my eye. The headline reads: "Missing son of Jewel tycoon found dead."

Michael Brant, only son of Hugh Brant, owner of the biggest diamond distributor in the state. The nineteen-year-old went missing six months ago. I scan the paragraph. Found in an alley across town, cause of death unclear. Possibly heart trauma. There it is, the part that caught my eye. "Strange burn mark across palm of left hand." It could be a coincidence, it most likely is. "The cause of the injury is unclear." It was assumed at first that the boy ran off. But if so, he didn't take anything with him. No clothes, no money. When a month went by the reward money started being offered, the search parties organized. Two months, no word. Three months, four...

They called it a possible kidnapping, but there was never any ransom demand. "Odd," I muse out loud.

The phone rings. I ignore it. Most calls I get these days are bill collectors, and the odd person who wants a job done. Always the same jobs, typical low-level detective work. They call me because of my reputation from my days in the force, and I turn them down every time. This time, after about the twelfth ring, I start to wonder if they'll give up. After the twentieth, I give up. Slapping my newspaper down atop a precarious pile, I cross the room and lift the handset to my mouth. "'Lo?"

"Mr. Drake?" The voice is British and professionally dry.

"Who's asking?" I've already figured this is a collection agency, but I've gone and answered the phone, might as well know before I hang up on this schmuck.

"Detective Ethan Drake?"

I haven't been a detective in ten years. Would a debt collector call me thas? "Yes, yes, now what do you want?"

"Mr. Drake, this is Mr. Weston, calling from I.E.S. We were referred to you specifically. We hope that you can help us in regard to a...delicate situation."

I.E.S: Integrated Energy Systems. The parent company of CoilTech. I.E.S invented and owns the Coil, making them the most powerful organization in the state. This day isn't starting out good.

"Sorry, can't help you," I say despite my burning curiosity. The biggest emerging energy company in the world, calling a retired street cop. This has to be something big. No. I move the receiver from my ear, determined to slam it down and walk away.

"A Ms. Ezla gave me your name, sir; she was very adamant that we call you, and only you."

As soon as I hear the name, I'm glued to the receiver. Good or not, today certainly isn't starting out boring. I can't let off how curious I am, though. I want him to work to convince me, let slip as much as possible before I make a decision. "Well, I'm not sure what she told you, but I'm retired, have been for a long time."

"So I've been led to understand, Detective Drake. But we were hoping you'd consult with us on this one matter."

"Look, buddy. For one, you can drop the 'Detective' crap, I quit. Two, I don't even know what this is about yet. I'm not about to drag my ass across town in rush hour traffic to find out I'm being called in to bust some kid for graffiti. I'm a busy man, so make this quick." That last part's a lie, but this chump doesn't need to know that. Neither does Lin Ezla, for that matter. How many years has it been? Eight, nine since we last talked? I don't regret it anymore per se; enough time goes by and you stop self-pitying over the past. Still, it's got my interest piqued.

"Well we've had some...I'll just call them breaches in our security for now. It's raised some safety concerns."

"Alright, but why call me?"

"We are also under a small degree of pressure to resolve the issue internally, rather than have the public police force spend resources."

It's one perk about owning virtually all the electricity in the city. Since all police vehicles and weapons, as well as the energy for government facilities, switched to CoilTech technology, I.E.S is allowed to run their own investigations when it comes to possible criminal activity on their property, to preserve company secrets and maintain the structural integrity of the ever so precious machine. What I'm getting from this dustcloud's wording is that something big's gone down, something the police are itching to get their paws into.

"What kind of security breaches?" I'll keep baiting the bastard, even though I know I'm not getting anything too specific, not over the phone. Something's going on that I.E.S wants to keep very quiet.

"Mr.Drake, if you could just come by, we'll brief you the full details. We could really use your help."

"And what do I get out of helping you?"

"The company is willing to compensate you substantially for the trouble, if you can help us solve our issue. The starting offer I've been told to quote to you is one hundred thousand in international credits."

International credits, currency with a value immune to exchange rates, taxes, or inflation. That kind of cash can go a long way, worldwide. Whatever this situation of theirs is, it's bad. "Sorry, no can do, not without some idea of what I'm looking at."

"Sir, please."

"Bye," I slowly lower the receiver.

"There's been a death."

I pause. "What kind of death?"

"If you'd just come down to I.E.S—"

"A death in the CoilTech facility?!" I'm not even trying to hide my interest now.

"Y-yes."

"I'll be there in an hour." I slam the receiver down. From my bedside drawer I pull out my pistol, encased in its worn leather holster. The weapon's been left untouched for years except for a semi-annual cleaning. Even when I was in the force it pushed the line of legality. All police weaponry was replaced by CoilTech tasers a while back, and lethal force has long been outlawed. The stainless-steel revolver is an antique. I only get away with it because of its custom ammunition. Right now, I have it loaded with three basic rubber bullets, a stick charge gel taser, a tracker, and an expanding foam unit. I just don't feel like I'm at work without this old cannon by my side.

The train rattles and shakes under my feet. I'm a broke bastard, no mistake, but not so broke that I need to use public trains to get around. There's a beat up old car in the parkade of my building. Heck, even *that* runs on a CoilTech energy receiver. But trains help me think.

To this day, CoilTech either hasn't perfected a train engine, or they haven't managed to buy out the contracts from companies still producing old-school steam engines. It isn't far in coming, though. CoilTech may not have its claws in the engineering side of public transport, but it managed, over two decades ago, to get all trains running on its smartware. Everything from guidance systems to temperature control, very little remains in this city that isn't dependent on CoilTech. And the ground is shrinking under anyone trying to resist progress.

The train is silent but for an occasional cough or sleepy mumble. I stand with one hand on the overhead railing, my hat pulled down low to shade my eyes from harsh lights above.

A TV screen mounted on the far wall flickers with black and white images from behind scribbled graffiti as a female reporter gives the latest news on Iran, the most recent country to join the swell of nations which have signed contracts with the U.S in exchange for the promise of CoilTech. Where our government ends and I.E.S begins is becoming less and less clear. It's like the world is up for sale, and CoilTech is the universal price. I turn my attention to the window, and see the Coil, like a massive glowing centerpiece to the city, disappearing into the gray clouds that overcast the sky.

Of course, it all hinges on good old New York. We're the first, and so far, the only city to use I.E.S technology as our main power source. Legal issues prevented I.E.S from releasing CoilTech to the world without a testing period of fifty years. So, they went big, using one of the largest cities in the world to prove just how safe and reliable the Coil is. At the end of this year, the testing period is up. Just a few months before every major city on earth sports its own big glowing bug zapper.

That thought didn't always leave such a bad taste in my mouth. I'm pushing forty, which means I've spent my entire life in a city with Coil energy at the forefront. By the time I joined the force in my twenties, everything from weapons to radios to vacuum cleaners were powered via remote energy from that glowing tower. "A utopia of clean and limitless energy." I heard those words so often, saw the ubiquitous slogans across so many posters and billboards, that for most of my life I've taken it for a given that this technology really would bring us to a brighter future.

Ten years ago I was made to doubt that, and now, I see Paradise rotting from the inside. With the steady advance of CoilTech into multiple facets of industry, factories as well as toll booths and other service stations are automated. Unless you own shares in the company, work for them, were born into money, or are lucky enough to have held onto one of the dwindling jobs left, you're screwed. "Limitless, free energy." Except free is a misnomer. The fuel cells sold to other nations from the excess power of the Coil make the government and I.E.S a tidy profit, along with payoffs from partnering nations chomping at the bit for the revolutionary technology. It helped us out of the Depression, but in these streets, I've seen neighborhoods where you'd think the bad days never ended.

I brood as the train speeds through tunnels and over bridges, gray stone blurring by. And always the Coil comes back to my line of sight, as if it's the sun and Manhattan its solar system. This is already the closest I've been to the damn thing in ten years. I can't deny feeling like there's some sort of unfinished business there. A feeling like I should revisit that place where I lost faith in my career and let my life go to hell. It's a feeling I've been good at ignoring. Until now.

I step off the train onto a grimy platform. Already I feel a slight electric tingle, like static, making the hairs on my arms and neck stand up. Experts insist this feeling is purely psychological, that the Coil's energy is both invisible and intangible until it connects with one of its receivers. Paranoid schmuck that I may be, even I'm willing to admit that maybe it's all in my head.

I avoid looking at the light as I descend the stairs out of the station. Instead I focus on following a haphazard trail of people walking to the double door entrance to I.E.S, the circular structure that forms a ten-story wall around the

Coil. The doors slide open to reveal a small lobby with white walls and little else. People stand lined up in front of a large gray metal door at the other end of the room, scanning keycards on a small glowing window one by one and stepping through as the door opens. I idly wonder what happens when someone tries to sneak in behind an employee without his or her own card.

I turn my attention to a service window off to the side. A sign above it reads "Visitor registration." A square faced woman sits on the other side amid a cloud of cigarette smoke, reading a magazine. No automated greeting machine for I.E.S headquarters, I suppose. I step over and tap the counter. The smoker puts her rag down with an exaggerated sigh and croaks through the intercom: "Welcome to I.E.S; how can I help you?"

"Drake, I'm expected." I wait while she sifts through pages in a massive logbook. A gaudily painted fingernail slides down a page. She nods before sliding it across to me through a gap in the window. "Sign here and mark the time. Right now, it's—"

"I got it," I fish out my pocketwatch, a large piece made of tarnished brass on a brass chain. Older than the Coil, older than me. Analog watches and clocks are a thing of the past, replaced by CoilTech digital timepieces. I like things old fashioned. I write the time down next to my name. "So which way do I go?"

"Detective Drake?"

Hearing the voice come from behind me, I spin around faster than I can think, reaching under my coat. I stop halfway through pulling my revolver free.

The man is in his late fifties, with short-cropped gray hair that's balding in the front. Dark eyes peer out from a wrinkled face behind small round spectacles. "Detective? It's Weston, we talked earlier," same British voice. He holds out a hand to shake mine.

Slowly, I ease my hand away from the gun. "Ethan, or Mr. Drake if you have to be formal about it. Not detective, not anymore."

Weston nods with a polite smile. A section of wall is missing behind him, presumably where a sliding door was made to blend into the lobby wall. The hag behind the service window must have pressed a button somewhere. "Were you waiting in there for me all damn morning?"

Another polite smile. "You are a very important guest today Dete—Mr. Drake. There is much to discuss. Please, follow me." Weston turns and walks into the secret doorway. I hesitate a moment, then follow. Inside is a tiny room with an elevator at the other end. A small metal table is positioned to the right, with an I.E.S security guard behind it.

"If you'd please leave any and all weapons here," Weston says with a gesture. "Then we can proceed."

"Not happening," I growl.

"Mr. Drake, I'm afraid it's company policy for your safety as much as ours."

"You can shove your policy. You don't call in a cop and then take his gun at the door. That's not how this works, bud."

Mr. Weston retains his calm, but when he responds, it's with a decided coolness. "If I recall, you were quite insistent on saying you are retired. All guests here, regardless of job or station, go by the same rules."

"Then you can forget my help. No one's getting my piece, end of story."

After a few tense moments go by. Finally, Weston nods. "Very well." He presses a button and the elevator doors slide open. "This way."

The ride down is longer than I expect. Not

surprisingly, the I.E.S facility is larger than it appears. When the elevator stops and the doors open, I'm faced with a gray-walled hallway with a lime green linoleum floor, lit by harsh fluorescents. Our footsteps echo down the passage. Near the end, Mr. Weston turns to a door on the left and opens it, stepping aside with a gesture for me to go in first.

Patting the holstered gun under my coat for reassurance, I step inside. Lights flicker on to illuminate the dark room, and I gasp. My breath mists in front of me in refrigerated air. On metal slabs in neat rows, lie at least two dozen corpses. What the hell have I got myself into...

"You're early, for a change," comes a crisp voice. I turn to find myself face to face with Lin Ezla. My ex-wife. She walks into the room, black high heels clacking rhythmically on the floor, brunette curls bouncing with each step. And abruptly I'm being held in a tight hug, feeling the contours of her lithe, muscular body pressed against mine. With a kiss on the cheek she breaks the hug, caressing the side of my face with a cool, slender hand. "You need a shave." Her smile is warm, and stunning. "I've missed you."

For a moment a half-strangled grunt is all I can manage. I somehow forget the cadavers filling the chilled room. When I remember, I step away from her with a shudder. "Lin, what on earth is going on here? I was expecting *one* stiff, not twenty. This is big, too big even for your bosses to keep under wraps."

"Which is exactly why I gave them your name. If you can figure this out, stop this from happening again, we can avoid this going public. I.E.S can move forward in the new year as a worldwide sustainable energy source. I know that's not necessarily what you want," she continues. "But you're the best man for the job. You'll have all the credits you need, and maybe even answers. Closure, a chance to leave the past behind you where it belongs."

Answers. She's got me there. A hook better than her looks or her boss's money. Answers to a decade old question that's haunted me. If I can find out what happened back then, I can expose I.E.S. Such a young girl, dead. And these bastards covered it up, pressured my superiors to keep it hushed. "What if I say no and walk away, seeing what I've seen?"

Lin shakes her head ruefully, biting her lip in that way I remember. "Ethan, my dear, who would believe you now? You're not exactly a credible witness."

She's right. Alcoholic ex-cop, vs. I.E.S? I wouldn't have a leg to stand on.

"Here," Lin pulls a thick manila file from her handbag and hands it to me. "Look through this." The woman knows I've made up my mind. I'm taking the case. I pace among the corpses, flipping through the file. Photos, reports, missing person posters. I glance from photos to cadavers and back. The victims are all over the spectrum, from barely adolescent teens to middle aged men and women; from business moguls to homeless addicts. Black and white and everything in between. My breath mists before me as I pace through the macabre freezer. Mr. Weston and Lin watch in silence. The deceased have but one common feature. Burn marks spiraling from the left palm up across the forearm. And when I turn a body over, using my coat sleeves as gloves, I find a spot on the back of the neck to match.

I speak, seeing Lin almost jump from the corner of my eye as I continue to stare at the stiff in front of me. "So when you found the Brant kid dead, whose idea was it to dump him in an alley?" Weston covers his gasp with a false cough. I look first him, then Lin, in the eyes. "Is this the promising career you wanted? I'm surprised your bosses didn't just hide his death like they did these poor saps, or could Hugh Brant not be bought off?"

Weston stammers in protest, but I keep my gaze intent on Lin. His voice might as well be television static in the background.

Lin's reply is so cool and detached, I start to wonder if I even know who she is anymore. "Hugh Brant and his wife agreed to silence, under the condition that their son's body be made available to them for burial."

Suddenly, the part of this whole thing that confused me most is the only part that makes sense. It would be ludicrous to dump one body where it could be found, while keeping the rest hidden. Unless the victim's family had some way of knowing, or at least suspecting, the company's involvement. They couldn't miraculously produce the corpse of their missing son, which explained why the corpse was arranged to be found the way it was. "But why? Why would they agree to stay quiet? This can't be legal, even for you people."

"There's no foul play here, Ethan. Any legal liabilities are ours to deal with, and will not affect you. I promise."

I sigh. "Suicide again, right? Don't give me that crap, Lin. There's more to this and I think you know it. Besides, even if I.E.S is allowed its own internal investigations department, that doesn't make it legal for you to dump bodies around the city." I realize I'm clenching my fist on the file, crumpling it. "How? How was this allowed to happen again? I thought security was doubled after what happened to the girl."

"These people...We believe they're operating as a group, a cult of some sort. It's always one at a time, every week—"

"Jesus, Lin! How long have you been keeping these stiffs frozen here?"

Lin steps closer and lowers her voice. "Ethan, my employers want you to do one thing, and one thing only. Track this group and report their location so we can stop this from continuing. That's it, that's all."

"So much for my answers," I mutter with a sneer I can't suppress.

Lin shakes her head almost imperceptibly, her eyes flickering to the right, to Mr. Weston. That warning look in her eyes means be quiet.

I take the file with me when I leave. There's so much buzzing through my head, so many pieces that I know fit together, even if I can't fathom how. So I start from what I do know.

I drive uptown to the Brant estate, a monolith of antique red brick and statuesque marble, with intricate fountains and sculpted hedges dotting the massive front yard. I park half a block up and walk my way back to the house. Naturally, it's fenced off by thick iron bars. I work my way around to the back, careful to stay behind neat trees and bushes, taking care not to be seen by the guard sitting in a booth beside the double gate. In the rear I find a service entrance, a small single door leading out to an equally small gate, for trash to be brought out and supplies brought in.

The estate sits on a rare bit of land not overrun with crammed-together buildings, and sports a small copse of trees behind it. I squat down against a tree and wait. While I do this, I go through the file some more, looking for connections. One death a week, all on Sunday nights, all around the same time, between midnight and two A.M. I notice something else. While the older victims are from all across the social and financial spectrum—in fact mostly between lower and middle class—the younger ones all share a commonality. Every one of them comes from a background of affluent wealth, or from a family with business connections to I.E.S. It could be nothing, but it brings me to question the suicide cult theory. If senior members were recruiting young rich kids, they certainly wouldn't be going to meet their makers first. People who recruit others into these kinds of things either want to die with their followers en masse, or not at all. It just doesn't fit.

Iron creaks against iron, and I jump to my feet. One of the cleaning staff is bringing bags out to a locked metal dumpster pressed against the fence. Carefully, I step out of the shadow of the trees as the aproned woman fumbles with the dumpster's lock. Moving as quickly and silently as I can, I slip through the service gate and through the door.

I pass the kitchen and laundry rooms, then through a nondescript door into the house proper. It's lavishly decorated, with a floor of shining marble and a spiraling staircase of polished oak. I ignore the paintings and statues and dash upstairs, hoping I don't get spotted. I feel my blood pumping hot through my veins. The thrill of the chase, I haven't felt it in ages, and I can't deny how good it feels. Cautiously, I peek into the rooms. An office, a lounge. Finally, I find what I think I'm looking for. A bedroom, still opulent but too small to be the master suite, with sports trophies and framed awards decorating the walls. I step in. When the maid straightens up from where she'd been dusting, I freeze at the same time as she does. We stand, silently, and I think my eyes must be almost as wide as hers. "Policia," I say softly, raising a hand. Her eyes go wider if anything, and shift around as if looking for others. "I...I'm no supposed to talk to you. You can't be here."

"I'll make it quick, it's important. I need to know what you can tell me about Michael, what was he like, before he disappeared?"

"I no supposed to say." She looks scared.

I sigh and pull out a small stack of bills I brought. *One hundred thousand international credits,* I remind myself as I hold out the money. The maid cranes her neck to peer over my shoulder, then quickly snatches the bills. There goes my rent. "He acted strange, not right."

"What do you mean?"

"He stayed in room, and when he came out, he spoke very little. And..." she hesitates.

"And what?"

"Things started to happen around him. Bad things. Dog dead, glass breaking without being touched. Light flickering, power on and off. I was...I was scared of him."

"Did he ever mention anything out of the ordinary? Anything new that may have happened to him?"

She shakes her head frantically.

"Are you sure?"

She nods.

"Ok. Go, continue your work. I'm going to look around the room for a minute, then I'll see myself out."

She walks out at something close to a run, and I ease the door closed behind her. I need to do this quickly. There's no telling if the petty cash I gave the maid will buy her silence. I open drawers in the massive oak dresser, rifling through clothes. Nothing. I check the closet, I check the nightstand and under the bed. My questing fingers feel under the mattress and touch on something. A small leather book, a journal. I flip it open to a random page. The handwriting is all over the place, completely erratic.

The defective one will set us free.
The defective one will set us free.
The defective one will set us free.

It's the same message, over and over, page after page,

scrawled in massive letters and jotted in miniscule print throughout the journal. I can't make heads or tails of it.

I'm almost too distracted by the journal to take note of the sound of boots in the hallway. When I realize what I'm hearing, I curse under my breath. The maid must have gone straight to security. I dash to the window and fling it open. There's a two story drop below, but decorative vines cling to the wall. The doorknob behind me turns. I swing myself out and grab hold of the vines just as the guards burst into the room. I climb halfway down before my foot slips, and my weight tears the vines free.

The fall knocks the air out of my lungs. I let out a heavy grunt of pain, rolling over. Nothing's broken, but my back's going to be bruised all kinds of interesting colors. An alarm sounds. I rise to my feet and hobble across the lawn, back to the service gate. A guard runs toward me, raising his taser. In one smooth motion I draw my pistol and fire. The shock round hits him and he goes down, unconscious. I get clear of the gate and run. My legs feel like they're on fire by the time I stop to catch my breath. I take on a neutral pace once I reach the road, walking as if I don't have a care in the world. The journal is tucked safely in my coat pocket, whatever good it'll do me.

Bourbon helps numb my bruised back, but it doesn't do much for my thoughts. I'm back at my apartment, staring at the open book on my table, swigging straight out of the bottle. Not a single address, not a single name or number. No personal revelations, no clues. The book has nothing in it to lead me to this so-called cult. The file is spread open beside the journal. If the pattern continues, it means there'll be another death tonight. The best way to track these people is to start at I.E.S, but obviously they're good enough at what they do to avoid even the best security systems. So, what chance do I have?

In the file are included reports from I.E.S investigators who tried tracking the group before me. Accounts of electronic devices suddenly going haywire, or shutting down entirely, as soon as the investigators felt they were getting close. Accidents, like street lamps falling over, or cars rolling onto the sidewalk. Over the last three days I've followed up with every source I have, called every informant, and turned up nothing.

I chuckle, feeling the numbing sensation of drunkenness creep over me. For a little while, I really thought I could do something. This time, I believed I could stop it from happening again. The girl's face swims in my mind, that eerily calm smile just before she touched the glowing surface of the Coil. I drain the bottle and hurl it against the far wall, where it strikes and clatters to the floor, unbroken. There's nothing I can do. Nothing.

I hardly realize what I'm doing when I load a bullet into my revolver to replace the one spent on the guard at the Brant estate. I take a small copper ring out of my drawer, which has several wires folded around it, and a small silver batter attached. A pre-CoilTech silencer. Antique, and very illegal. I slide it onto the gun, and it contracts onto the barrel with a snap, beeping to indicate it's active. Then, I'm strapping my shoulder holster on and donning my coat. It'll be sundown soon, and I want to be in position as early as possible.

The sky remains gray and clouded, threatening rain. I drive down twisting back lanes and through industrial neighborhoods until I find myself under the glow of the Coil, waiting in a shadowed alley facing the wall of I.E.S headquarters. I sit and wait. As it gets later, I drive around, making a circuit around the Coil without being in direct view of the facility. I catch glimpses of uniformed guards patrolling at street level and atop the building. I park in a different alley, wait some more. Rinse and repeat, until it's all etched into my brain in full detail. This part of town, at this time of night on a Sunday, there are hardly any pedestrians, and none matching the descriptions of any missing persons, whose faces I've done my best to study in the time I've had. I don't know what I hope to accomplish that the guards can't, and I call myself an idiot for being here. But I sit and wait all the same.

The few gulps I take from my flask are enough to make the time slip by easier without taking away my edge. Hours pass. I time the guard's patrols. He does a circuit every half hour. Parked not too far down from the guard entrance, I watch the steel door. It's shut tight, equipped with a scanner for access cards.

When my watch strikes midnight, I still haven't seen anything. Rain taps a drumbeat on my windshield. The guard arrives at the security door and goes inside. I'm just about ready to start driving around again when something catches my eye. A flash of blue electrostatic light along the wall of I.E.S. I open my door and lean out, looking up. Dark shapes rise up as though carried by lightning, darting over the top of the facility, leaping from the roofs of buildings across the street. Before I know what I'm doing, I'm running for the security door. I sway, realizing I may have drunk too much after all. But I definitely just saw what I saw, insane as it may be.

Things started to happen around him. The maid's words replay in my mind. I slip and crash shoulder first into the door, slamming my fist against the cold steel and hollering at the top of my lungs. When the guard cautiously opens the door he finds the barrel of my pistol in his face. I grab his taser and toss it out into the rain. "You have intruders," I say breathlessly. I grab his keycard. "Move." I shove him ahead of me through the gray corridors. "I need to get to the Coil."

"You're insane. If you do get out of here, it'll be in cuffs."

"The Coil!"

"You wanna die? Do you have any idea what kind of power output it has right now? This time of the week, no one goes near it."

"Why?"

"Because this is when the spare power gets harvested into the fuel cells for shipping. Touching it will kill you, hell, going close to it could kill you."

"That's why I'm here. Keep walking." I shove the barrel into the back of his head. Around a corner ahead of us, another guard emerges. He cries out and fumbles for his weapon. I blast him with a rubber bullet to the hand, knocking the taser away, then hit him with a foam cap, pinning him to the wall. The lights flicker. No, not yet. We move faster, rounding one corner after another, until we stand before another door.

"Stay here." I hit my captive guard with a gel charge to the feet, simultaneously sticking him to the floor and incapacitating him with an electric current.

The keypad beeps when I swipe the card, and the door swings inward just as I hear a shout from behind. I dash through, ducking in time to avoid being hit by blue flashes from a taser gun. I spin around to see a guard rushing at me. A sheet of light appears out of nowhere, and he falls with a scream.

I guess now I know what happens if you forget to swipe in.

I turn around and freeze. I'm in the central courtyard, its center dominated by the Coil. Its glow casts shadows off the fuel cells lined up before it. Rain pelts the glass roof, and when I take a slow step my boots crunch on broken shards. Raindrops splash on my face as I look up to the stormy sky. It's only when I look down again that I see them.

They stand in a row, forming a semi-circle around the Coil, slivers of darkness on the backdrop of its pulsating light. And even though I can't see their eyes, I know all twelve of them are looking right at me.

In my mind, I've traveled ten years back in time, to that night. To that girl and her dazzling, horrifying smile. To that pale, slim shadow, small and vulnerable in the face of the Coil's remorseless glow.

A dozen pairs of eyes follow my every step as I make my stumbling approach. I feel the tingle of electricity, stronger now. This time, I know it's not my imagination.

"The defective one."

"Will set us free."

"We must find him."

They talk in turns, one after the other, in the same flat tone.

"The defective one will set us free," they say, all at once.

Suddenly my throat is very dry, and I wish I hadn't left my flask in the car. "You don't have to do this," I shout. "Whatever you've been told, whatever you believe, it's not worth dying for."

"Only the defective one can free us," says a member of the group.

"Do not interfere," chimes in another another.

"I'm here to help you. Let me help you find what you're looking for. Please."

"Do not interfere," all of them in unison again.

I hit an invisible wall. With a shout I shove myself forward, only to be bounced back. When I lunge forward again, the air crackles with blue static and I'm flung away to land on my back, body tingling. I get up, holding my pistol in a shaky hand. The group has turned towards the Coil. One of them is stepping closer to it as they chant.

"No!" I make another mad dash while their backs are turned. They've taken their attention off me, and the force that pushed me back has gone with it. I manage to grab the one approaching the Coil and fling him away. It's only now that I realize how close I am to the thing. Every last inch of my skin crawls with a static charge, like a million needles poking into me at once.

"Do not interfere," they say.

I feel a slash of pain across my chest, and then another, as though I'm being hit with invisible whips. I fire my gun, but the rubber bullet deflects from its target with a flash of light. Then my gun flies out of my hand and hits the Coil with a crackle.

The fuel cells start to shift, dragging across the concrete, towards the Coil. I feel a tug in my pocket, and when I look I see my watch floating out, toward the wall of light behind me.

"We must find the defective one."

"I don't know what you mean! Help me understand!"

I grab the watch instinctively, and it pulls me along with it, toward the Coil. I fumble with the other hand to unlatch the chain. It snaps off my coat and tangles around my arm, digging painfully into my skin. I'm pulled with it, hand first, to touch the wall of blinding light, and my world becomes pain, becomes burning agony as the power courses through me.

Then, everything goes black.

><del> <del><

"Your drink, sir?"

I take the bourbon from the server with mumbled

thanks. The good stuff, now. With a hundred grand in credits, I can afford it. I glance out at the ocean. I'm on a cruise liner, headed for...Well, wherever I want. I sip the drink and look again at the spiral mark on my left forearm. Like a burn that happened on the inside, which is essentially what it is. On the back of my neck is a similar mark.

After the pain of touching the Coil, I awoke to find cops and paramedics crawling all over I.E.S headquarters, and Lin standing by my stretcher as I was lifted into an ambulance. Apparently, one of the guards I took out went ahead and called the police.

The things Lin told me were hard to swallow at first, but as she explained it, it started to make more and more sense. CoilTech, the bastards. Barely a decade into their operations with the Coil they started dabbling in behavior modification technology, testing integrated receivers in orphaned infants. I guess pills are too outdated for some fat cats, because after a testing phase, I.E.S started selling this new tech to wealthy parents, all the while making them sign gag orders in case things went wrong. Which is, of course, what happened.

I guess they lost the paperwork on the early test subjects along the way, otherwise they never would have hired me to investigate the case. I now know the real reason I quit the force, or at least part of it. The radio waves feeding into my brain were designed to steer me away from acting against I.E.S. I guess it only partially worked.

Those other poor souls, they were drawn to the damn thing and they had no idea why, all they knew was that if a faulty unit was brought closer to the source, it would short circuit the whole system. They were fine, after I got zapped. But their memories of what happened after they snapped were gone. Luckily, the cops had more than enough evidence, with the Children of the Coil and the corpses in the freezer combined. Children of the Coil, that's what the news headlines are calling them.

As for why I didn't die, beats me. Maybe it's because I was one of the earlier prototypes. A defective one, as the Children said.

Lin cooperated with the police, as much as she could without incriminating herself. One thing she managed was to get my pay wired to me before the company went down. I.E.S is facing lawsuits from both the feds and the families of the Children, their former clients who claim they were extorted into selling out their newborn offspring. CoilTech is still in operation, taken over by the U.S government to complete the deal for the end of the year. All this crap, and the Coil is still going worldwide. I, for one, plan on being somewhere far away when that happens.

With a sigh, I reach for my bourbon. Blue static flashes briefly between my hand and the glass, and it slides across the table into my hand. The lights overhead flicker.

I chuckle, mirthlessly, and finish my drink.

Kaffeklatsch with Manuel Royal

and Andrew McCurdy

Andrew: Welcome to the Gallery of Curiosities, Manuel, and thank you for agreeing to sit down to this interview. As I was reading your story, *This Particular Evening*, I felt as though I needed some Louis Armstrong or Duke Ellington playing in the background. Do you ever listen to music when you write, or do you like to be free of distractions?

Manuel: I'm in favor of music. I stand by that statement, regardless of what backlash it might bring.

When I'm planning a major writing project (and that's where all the major ones are, in various stages of planning), I put together a musical playlist for it, and always imagine having it as a continuous soundtrack while I tap-tap some pure genius onto the page. In reality, when I try to make writing and music a simultaneous experience, either I focus on the work and block out the music entirely, or—more likely—I find myself listening to lyrics instead of finding my own words.

So I listen to music before trying to write. Sometimes to get in a mood appropriate to the piece (as you suggested, I listened to a lot of 1920s music—Louis Armstrong, Ruth Etting, Bessie Smith, Earl Hines—while thinking about *This Particular Evening*). And sometimes just to reactivate my emotions and reconnect with an idea that's gone flat and stale in my mind.

But the only way I can seem to focus and actually get the work done is to shut out all distractions. Sometimes wearing earplugs.

Andrew: The names, *Joey Epilogue* and *Quick Dip Bitsy,* really seem to fit the personality of the two protagonists. How did the development of those two characters progress from an idea to the page?

Manuel: That was spontaneous. I don't really have a conscious process for constructing a character. There's a slot open, a character shows up, and I gradually see them more clearly via their actions and words. Especially dialogue. Once I get characters talking to each other, the shape of the story begins to appear to me. Maybe it's like a bat's echolocation in a cave.

With this particular story, the style of names, dialogue, and most of all narration are my inadequate homage to Damon Runyon. I was thinking about his distinctive "perpetual present tense" and thought of applying it to a time travel story.

Andrew: What are you working on now?

Manuel: My first serious attempt at a novel since I was a teenager; to be called *Les Familiers.* I guess it would be categorized as urban fantasy, being set in contemporary Atlanta (where I live) and featuring, for better or worse, three animal protagonists and some pretty strange humans doing extranormal things through mysterious means of unknown origin and mechanism. Embarrassing to say, it came to me in a dream. Occasionally the subconscious, shuffling through the detritus of a brain on the wash & rinse cycle, slaps together something usable.

Andrew: What role does research play in your writing?

Manuel: For a story like *This Particular Evening,* I usually have most of what I need in my head thanks to decades of directionless reading of works of popular history. Our friend the Internet lets me nail down particular details.

But for a longer work, I might do three hours of research for every hour of actual composition. And there's where the Internet becomes a vast warren of rabbit holes, and sometimes a wild goose chase, and then there's a chicken-or-the-egg deal. Lot of animals involved. Chicken/egg meaning that a complex story requires research, and research inevitably leads to serendipitous discoveries that suggest other stories.

The process makes it a mathematical certainty that the measured ranks of back burners in my mind, each bearing a putative future project, will always grow faster than I can hope to deal with them, and no matter how many stories I write, I'll die with a greater number intended but unaccomplished, evaporating into limbo.

Andrew: What is your process for editing your work once you have finished a draft?

Manuel: Usually what happens, is I save a backup copy of the file, then immediately go back through it, paragraph by paragraph in reverse order, revising as I go, then skim in through forwards again to see if it still makes sense. Then I print it and let my girlfriend read it. She inevitably finds a typo or two that I've missed.

I've proofread professionally, and constantly find errors in published books. Yet anybody can miss their own errors, even multiple times. There's nothing like having another pair of eyes take a look. And not just eyes, but taste. There's no accounting for taste, but also no dispensing with it. It lets you distinguish quickly between cotton candy and fiberglass insulation.

Andrew: How often do you read for pleasure, and what do you look for when you read the works of other authors? Conversely, what are some of your pet peeves about works you have not enjoyed?

Manuel: I usually can't get to sleep without reading at least a little. And sometimes a book will hook me so well I stay with it for hours at a stretch—one of life's great pleasures. But more and more it feels like there's never enough time, and I know in a given year in this 21st century of ours I read a mere fraction of the number of books I read in a year of my youth. Most of us spend more time staring at screens than we do looking at paper pages now. Of course, we do read stuff on those screens, but it's not the same experience.

I look for exciting ideas, for worlds I've never seen but want to visit (or that make me grateful I don't have to live there), and for strong characters. Not necessarily characters that are strong people, but well-drawn, convincingly realized characters with their own internal lives. I want honest emotions to emerge from the story without having to be spelled out.

Pet peeves—when it sounds like a writer's a little too in love with his own style. When characters do stupid things that make no sense solely to force the plot to happen. I won't name names.

Except for one name, because another pet peeve is when a writer insists on being Neil Gaiman. Why? Because Neil Gaiman is my Evil British Twin. The two of us were born on the same day—he on the island of Great Britain, me on the island of Key West. We've had a number of the same ideas, including one about Santa Claus, a.k.a. Father Christmas.

Yet we're at very, very different levels of success, mainly because Neil Effing Gaiman has cheated by working hard at his craft from an early age, which I was totally going to but got distracted.

Andrew: Perhaps we've had enough *kaffee* at this *klatsch*.

Manuel: The buttercream icing on that cupcake of bitter envy is that Mr. Gaiman, besides being an extraordinarily gifted storyteller who's earned all his success, appears to be a genuinely good person. He inspires me to try harder. Which is irritating. Maybe I'll switch to decaf.

Andrew: What do value the most in feedback and reviews from your readers?

Manuel: Brutal honesty.

Though—to be honest on my part—I don't really look for feedback and reviews. I guess I'll have to deal with that eventually. I've seen one seriously bad review for a story I did *("Heart-Shaped")*, by someone who didn't understand it at all. Unless—unless, he was actually an (even) older version of me, bitter and hateful like elderly Boccaccio, somehow transmitting his disdain back through time. It was on the Internet—hell, how can one know? Could be from the future.

Andrew: Finally, what do you enjoy most about being a writer?

Manuel: When I know I've used the right word, rather than the right word's second cousin. No—before that. When a spontaneous connection happens in my mind and something's there that's new. No—way, way after that, when a whole crap-ton of those connections have all been glued together with, oh, let's call it creative mucilage, and the mist clears and you see—well, nine times out of ten it's an appallingly unwholesome landfill, but just occasionally it's a place I call Fabulopolis. Like Disneyland, but better.

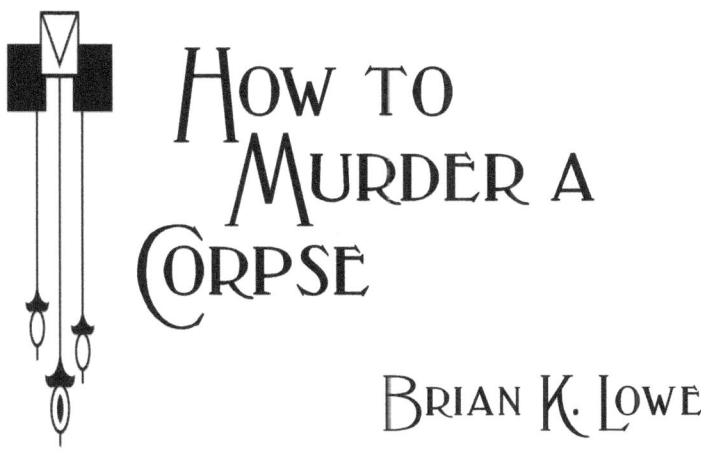

How to Murder a Corpse

Brian K. Lowe

SAMMY LAY SPRAWLED on the floor next to my client chair, a bullet hole in his forehead and two bite marks on his throat. Somebody had made damned sure he was dead past any hope of resurrection, even by one of those Ph.D.s in necromancy from some fancy Ivy League college, let alone a correspondence school hack like me. Which seemed a lot of work when you figured that I'd already raised Sammy from the dead last week.

L.A.'s got its share of vampires, and it's never been short of palookas with a gun and a temper, but this was over the top, even for Tinseltown.

Sammy had been one of my few friends. We'd gone to high school together, worked the same odd jobs, whistled at the same girls. I got my P.I. license, he got a real job. When the war came, Sammy spent four years in the Pacific, while I stayed home, for reasons he never brought up because he was my friend. Four years without a scratch, and he comes back to get clipped walking across Sunset

Boulevard—by a drunk cop, no less.

I resurrected him so he could wrap things up, testify at the trial, attend his own funeral. He knew it wasn't going to last, zombies never do. Now here he was in my office, dead again.

The same question kept chasing round and round my head, like a dog nipping at its own tail:

Why go to so much trouble to murder a walking dead man with maybe another week to go before he keeled over forever?

"I'm sure surprised to see you down here. I'd've thought you'd be stuck upstairs for hours."

"Sammy was dead already," I said. "I told 'em I didn't do it, but it's not like they really care."

Cy Guernsey wiped his hands on a towel before he answered. I appreciated his hygiene, even if Sammy, lying on his slab, didn't. Cy's not a real police surgeon, he just helps out. But he knows stuff, and none of those other guys will talk to me, so I make do.

"Not even with the bite marks? I'd'a thought the Night Squad would wanna know about that."

I gave him the kind of look you give cabbies when they want an extra tip just for tailing a mark around town.

"Cy, Sammy was run down last week by a car driven by Monte Buchalter. Monte Buchalter works on the Night Squad, and word is he was drunk that night. The cops weren't happy I brought Sammy back; how hard do you think they're going to look for whoever shot him?"

Shaking his head, Cy moved to another table, where his next customer waited. I stayed put, because Cy didn't like me near his "clients." It wasn't like I was going to try to resurrect any of them, but it probably creeped him out that I could. *If* I could. They were pretty dead by this point.

Almost as dead as Sammy.

"And there's no way you can bring Sammy back again to ask him what happened?"

I laughed. Better that than how I really felt. "I doubt it. Course, everything I know I learned from a phonograph record I got in the mail out of an ad I saw in the back of a magazine. I sent in twenty bucks and they sent me back the record and a really thin brochure. Memorize everything on the record, it said, and repeat it exactly, or you'll end up like the guy in the picture. Believe me, you didn't want to end up like the guy in the picture."

"That," he said, "is one unbelievable story."

"Hey, it's not like I'm the first guy to learn a trade through the mail."

"Yeah, but—damn, *you* shelled out twenty bucks?"

I gave him a "Why-I-oughta—" glare and changed the subject. Last thing I wanted was anybody asking why I got into this gig in the first place.

"So, Cy, you're looking pretty snazzy tonight. Hot date?"

Cy shrugged and grinned. He was wearing new shoes, and there were no stains on his pants. "You know how it is. You want to impress the ladies, you gotta look the part." He held up his wrist, his face lighting up like a kid on Christmas morning. "You see my new watch? A present."

"Wow. She must really like you."

His face clouded over. "What, you think I don't deserve stuff like this? Just 'cause you only come in when you want somethin'... I got a life, you know. Some people think I'm pretty hot stuff."

Time to change the subject again. My not having a social life didn't give me the right to razz Cy about his. I jerked my head toward Sammy. "So what killed him?"

"He got hit by a car. You said so yourself."

"No, I mean what killed him *this* time—the bullet or the vampire?"

"Oh. Well, that's what you want the M.E. for. But I think I can help you out a little." Now that Cy was back on the job, he was all business, pointing out Sammy's wounds as he talked. "A normal vamp won't touch a dead guy, of course; there's no life force, nothing for him to take. But Sammy's been drained of blood, and there's enough trace at the neck—" pointing—"that I can pinpoint the bites as the point of exsanguination." He looked up at me expectantly.

"Yeah, where the blood was drained. I know what it means. But why would a vampire bite a zombie? And what about the bullet hole?"

"Now that's where things get interesting," said the guy for whom vampire-bitten, head-shot reanimated zombies apparently weren't interesting enough. "According to the report, it was a .38 slug." Like the cops use, but he didn't want to say that. "There's no blood around the wound at all. That means the shot came post-mortem—or in this case, post-post-mortem." He frowned. "Post-mortem-post?" Then he saw the look on my face and got back to my friend lying on the slab. "Uh, after the bite, anyway."

"Zombies are pretty fragile. Even if a vamp would want to bite one, I wouldn't have thought it would survive. But if somebody shot Sammy *after* he lost his blood, I guess I was wrong." I shook my head. "This is beyond me. I need to talk to somebody, see if there's anything to be done."

Cy blinked. "You think you maybe *could* bring him back—again?"

"Nah, not me." I made a sour face. "But there is a guy..."

A shadow fell across the table. Cy jumped. I didn't; I'd heard Monte Buchalter's signature wheeze when he came in. Sometimes it's best not to show fear.

"What the hell is *that* doing out, and why the hell is *he* here?"

Cy was shaking in his boots, and I couldn't blame him. Buchalter was second-in-command of the Night Squad for a reason. He wasn't big, but he loomed. He had square shoulders, a square jaw, and a square head. There were rumors he'd gone into Germany ahead of the regular troops to deal with any surprises Herr Hitler's paranormal corps had set up. Alone. He was a hero.

A hero who'd killed my best friend. Time to get out of there.

"I—I thought you'd been sent home, Detective Buchalter," Cy said.

"Now that the victim can't testify, the DA's dropping the charges. I'm back on the job. I asked you a question, Guernsey. What is that doing out of its drawer?" He was pointing to Sammy's body, which he had just referred to as "that" for the second time. I should have gotten out while the getting was good.

"Sammy was my friend." I said it really low, because I was really close to Buchalter's face. I should have been scared, like Cy, because Buchalter was mean and tough and he was a cop in a town where mean and tough cops followed their own rules. But I was angry, and when I get angry, I get stupid, and I say things I later regret. "You ran him down in the street because you were too blind drunk to drive. Did you shoot him, too?"

I heard Cy suck in his breath.

"Watch your mouth." Buchalter kept his voice as low as mine. His breath was sweet, like he'd had breath mints for dinner. "It was an accident. You weren't there. And you ain't gonna raise him again, so I guess we'll never know what he says, will we?"

"You keep thinking that, Detective. And when Sammy

gets on that witness stand, you're going to look really stupid."

His eyes narrowed so slightly that I was only able tell because I was that close. His time on the Night Squad had made him familiar with the basics of necromancy, and as far as he knew, once was it. You don't come back a second time. But I knew more than just the basics, and now he wasn't so sure.

He recovered quickly. "Funny you should be hanging around. There's been a bunch of reports of jacked-up vamps attacking people at random. You wouldn't know anything about that, would you? Maybe we oughta go back upstairs and have a talk."

I had as little to do with vampires as possible and Buchalter knew it. But I've also been tossed out of enough joints to recognize the feeling. I backed off.

"Thanks, Cy. I'll let you know what I find out."

Popular opinion aside, there are people in this world sleazier than me. A lot of guys won't touch a corpse. Me, I don't do divorces. But at least I have a day job. Mac the Life, he kind of didn't. Mac will hire out to resurrect anybody—or anything. There's a rumor he once tried to give a vampire back his soul. Which means that even among the once-living, he's not considered proper dinner company.

But that doesn't change the fact that Mac knows more about life, death, and crossing the line in both directions than anybody. That, coupled with his willingness to sell his knowledge to whoever will pay him, had bought him a small house in the less-fashionable, but still expensive, section of Beverly Hills. One of these days, his work is going to kill him, but in the meantime, he enjoys himself. He looks like William Powell and sounds like Bette Davis.

We met in his living room, facing the pool he's never used.

"Been a while," he said, blowing cigarette smoke away from me. He's slimy, but polite.

"Not by accident, either." We'd been over what we thought of each other a long time ago. "I'm here about a client."

Mac nodded, smoke jetting from his lips. "I heard. Just when you think you've seen it all. A vampire-bitten zombie with a bullet in his head. Why would anybody do that?"

"It takes all kinds." *Just look in the mirror.* "I came to ask you a favor."

"A favor. I thought we weren't friends anymore."

"We aren't. Actually, we never were. But Sammy never had my good taste. He liked you, in spite of everything. The favor's for him."

Mac shrugged and puffed a smoke ring, the picture of a man in no hurry. I wondered if the cigarettes explained his voice.

"You know, it takes a certain kind of person to do what we do," he said to the ceiling. "And it's not what you're thinking. Anybody can read a recipe and raise a zombie, but it takes a little something 'extra' to do the job right. I've got it." He poked the cigarette at me. "You've got it, too. Something supernatural. Sometimes I know what's going to happen before it does. I bet you do, too, once in a while."

"Sure. It's what I like to call being a detective. You think you're psychic?"

"No...well, yes, maybe. But I got a feeling about Sammy, right after I heard about him being hit by that car. Like that was only one shoe, and there was another one waiting to drop. So I asked around. Turns out Sammy started hanging out at a vampire club downtown—after you brought him back. And now he turns up with bite marks."

I frowned. "What have zombies and vamps got in common?"

"I have no idea. Maybe if I do that favor for you, we can ask Sammy."

"Can you?"

He blew another smoke ring. "If I can't, nobody can. Why else would you come back here after all this time?"

"Only for Sammy," I said. "Give me the address." Before I left, I told him where he could find Sammy's body. I probably should have warned him about Buchalter, but they deserved each other.

The vampire club didn't have a name. Vamps are tolerated, in the main, but not well and not by everybody. They repay the favor by staying away from unwilling victims—in the main. Vamp clubs make that easier by providing a place where the biters can mingle with the wannabes. Like I told Mac, it takes all kinds.

The door wasn't locked, and there was no doorman, but it wasn't the kind of place you'd walk into by accident. I was carrying a flashlight in my coat pocket because vampire haunts are dark—why spend money on electricity if you don't use lights?—but I didn't need it; the narrow foyer was lit by a dusty ceiling fixture way up above my head. Steep stairs climbed to my right. Doctors and lawyers once had offices here; the directory was still hanging on the wall, but it was blank except for the legend that said 'Blish Professional Building.' At the end of the hall was a mesh elevator that descended at a rattling slow pace when I rang. I got in, closed the door, pressed the only button that wasn't covered in dust, and the car rose like a grandmother with two bad hips.

I started to hear a low rumble that I thought was the elevator getting ready to drop me four stories into the basement, but as I came even with my destination I realized it was music, throbbing bass tones from down the hall. Stepping out into the corridor, I saw lights coming from open office doorways. I had the feeling that those doctors and lawyers and accountants would never recognize this place now.

I walked up to the first doorway and peeked in. In spite of my earlier bravado, I moved like a guy taking pictures of a cheating husband. There was a reception area, with one of those sliding glass windows set in the opposite wall, the kind designed to keep patients from bothering the girls. I don't know what was going on behind the window, and it didn't matter. What was going on right in front of me stopped me in my tracks.

A vampire stood with his back to me, his head tilted to the right and slightly forward so he could sink his teeth into the neck of the man facing me, who showed no reaction to the fact that all of his blood was being drained.

The likely reason was that he was a zombie. All of a sudden a hand clamped onto my shoulder and I about hopped out of my skin.

"My, aren't we jumpy."

It was a vampire's hand, but he didn't seem angry or hostile; in fact he looked a little unfocused. His pupils were dilated, which I could have sworn was impossible for the undead. Could vampires use drugs? All of a sudden I wondered exactly what Mac had gotten me into. Regular vampires were paranoid and went to great lengths to preserve their privacy. What were doped-up vamps like?

The vampire, blond-haired and outwardly middle-aged, frowned and looked at me more closely. "You smell delicious." His voice was soft, like his face. He blinked. "You're *alive*. But there's the scent of the dead on you, as well." He looped an arm in mine and started to lead me down the corridor, shaking his head. "I have no idea what to make of you," he said genially. "I'll just take you to Angelo and let him figure it out. It's his turn anyway." I hadn't moved, and he tugged. "Come on. Let Uncle Leonard take you to Angelo."

I would get nowhere standing in the hall, so I let him bring me along. Not like I had a choice anyway. If he wanted me to go, he could make me. We strolled arm in arm to the last office, the one with the music that was making my head feel like somebody's bongo drum. Through the other open doorways, I saw the same scene over and over: vampires and zombies locked in obscene embrace. What either of them got out of it was beyond me. I must have passed close to a dozen, and who knows how many others were in back rooms. None of them took the slightest notice of me. It was as close as I have ever come to seeing Hell, and that's not an idle comparison.

"Angelo," my escort purred, "we have a visitor."

The booming bass came to an end as Angelo picked the needle up off the record. He looked like a 17-year-old James Dean, leather jacket and jeans, but his eyes were older. He gave me a look that was meant to scare me, but it only told me he was supposed to be watching for "visitors" while the rest of the vamps had their fun, and he wasn't happy that my being here unannounced showed he'd been loafing.

"Thanks, Leonard. I'll take it from here." Even his accent was peeved. Then he sniffed me, like Leonard had. He frowned, and then he smiled. "Oh...Leonard! You should have told me."

"I tried, Angie, but you never let me." Leonard took another whiff of me. And here I hadn't thought things could get any more creepy.

"Leave our guest alone, Leonard. He's not for you."

Angelo put his arm around my shoulders and lead me to a chair. The room held just two chairs and the desk that the phonograph was on. Another door lead to a file closet or maybe a private john. "So, you looking for work?"

"Yeah." No wonder they were treating me so well; they'd pegged me as a necromancer. I was starting to get the picture: They had a lot of zombies, but zombies don't last. They must have had at least one of us on payroll already, but two would be twice as good. "I was referred by a friend. He said you'd know who."

Angelo nodded, returning to his seat. "You got a name?"

"You can call me Mr. Riser." I'd used it before. There aren't so many necromancers in town that Angelo couldn't find me pretty easily, but I still didn't like the idea of my real name being tossed around in this place. "Where's your boss?" If Angelo was in charge, I'd eat my hat. "My friend was a little vague about exactly what I'm being hired to do."

Angelo got that look in his eye again, but this time it had some real scary in it. An angry vamp is a hungry vamp. His voice lost its waterfront bravado and descended into a low hiss.

"As far as you're concerned, blood-sack, I *am* the boss." He tried to lock his eyes on mine, but I was wise to that trick. "This is what you're doing here. We need zombies. You raise them. You tell them to come here. We pay you a hundred for every one. You keep your mouth shut."

Tough talk, but like I said, there aren't a lot of necromancers in town, and most of them weren't going to be found hanging out in seedy downtown vampire clubs. So these guys needed my skills, which meant I could afford to push a little. I stood up.

"Look, Angie. I came here because my friend said I could make some cash, but I don't have to stay.

Resurrecting people isn't easy, and finding clients..." A question had popped into my head, and I wondered if Angelo could answer it. At a C-note a head, raising as many zombies as I'd seen outside would be very profitable. But where did their guy get them? "Finding people to resurrect isn't easy in the first place. That's why my friend referred me. Said he couldn't keep up with demand."

Angelo just shrugged, his meanness retreating into himself.

"Near as I can tell, he's doing okay. I guess he's not so picky as you are about his clients. But that's between you guys. We can always use more product."

"So, any special kind of zombies you like? Unnatural deaths, virgins...?" I was flailing around, trying to find something to hold onto, something that would give me a clue where I could find my supposed "friend."

"Nah, doesn't matter. Dead's dead. Well, resurrected dead, I should say." Angie smiled so that he showed more fang than I'd ever wanted to see. He glanced around like we were planning some kind of heist, as if anybody was listening to us.

"Look, not a lot of people are in on this, but if you're gonna work with us, you need to know the score. We don't drink blood because we need it—we want the soul; living souls are like magic. But zombies—zombies are *made* of magic. It's way better than blood; it's like a drug, and guys will pay through the nose for it."

Like a drug. Buchalter had been so busy trying to keep Sammy from being evidence in his trial he couldn't see the clue right under his nose.

"But what about the zombies? What's in it for them?"

Angie relaxed into a chuckle. From him it did not sound funny.

"Zombies are stupid. They want to live so bad that they

arrange to be resurrected even when they know it's only gonna last a few days. They'll believe whatever you tell them." He leaned toward me. "You know how zombies can't go near dead animals?" I nodded. That was basic necromancy: A dead animal leeches the life out of a zombie. The bigger the animal, the worse it is. "Well, we just tell them that since we're *un*dead, being near us has the opposite effect. It makes them live longer. It doesn't, but it's not like they're around long enough to complain anyway."

Feeding vampires magic would bring the Night Squad on the double with stakes and torches. And if the zombies knew that the vamps couldn't extend their lives, they'd stop coming, maybe even go to the cops. Either way, the vamps lose their fix, and somebody's out a hundred bucks a zombie. Maybe Sammy had found out the truth, but what could he do? He couldn't very well go to the Night Squad. Was that why he'd come to my office? Had he been followed by Angie, or Leonard, or one of the vamps who was in the club that night?

On the other hand, it might have nothing to do with them. What if Buchalter had more on the ball than I thought? What if he'd been watching this place, and when he saw Sammy come out he figured he could kill two birds with one stone?

The telephone on the desk rang, and my nerves rang with it. I may not believe in psychic powers, but I *knew* that call wasn't a coincidence. It was bad news. I was moving for the door before Angelo said, "Hello?"

Vampires are fast. Really fast. If I ran, he'd grab me before I got to the end of the hall, and once he got his hands on me, I wouldn't stand a chance. I ducked into the first doorway off the hall and almost made myself a part of a very unpretty picture.

It was Leonard, and he wasn't alone. I heard Angie slam down the phone in the next office. There was no time to be polite. I grabbed Leonard's meal right out from under his fangs. Zombies aren't very strong, they only last a week or so. This one didn't have the strength to resist as I yanked him out into the hall.

Angelo came flying out of his office and slammed into the zombie. That look was back in his eyes, and an angry vamp is a hungry vamp. Face-to-face with a zombie already being bled, his instincts took over and he sank his teeth in the dead man's neck with a snarl.

I barely got out of the way before Leonard, his doughy face hard and angular with rage, burst from the room and tore into Angie, who'd stolen his prey. I didn't wait to see who won. I didn't wait to see what happened to the poor devil caught in the middle. I ran.

I didn't relax until I jumped onto a passing Red Car. I didn't think even a vamp could track me in a moving vehicle, so I used the time to think. That lasted as long as it took my ride to get within walking distance of Mac's house. He was the only one who'd known where I was going, the only one who could've ratted me out to Angie.

No lights showed in his neighbors' houses, but Mac's showed one, despite the late hour. I stood on the sidewalk. There was a gate to the backyard on the left that didn't look too sturdy, so I tried that way. That's when I found out I'd lost my flashlight. Damn. I was in dutch with the local vampires and here I was stumbling around in the pitch black. At least Mac didn't keep a lot of junk in his yard.

It had been hot lately, so I had more trouble getting through an open window than finding one. Creeping through Mac's darkened house, heading for the one light I had seen, I had time to debate how smart it was to confront him here on his home ground, and wonder whether he'd kept the gun he used on Sammy.

I had just enough time to ask myself why the best necromancer in Los Angeles needed a gun to stop a zombie when I found Mac and realized that this question, at least, had an answer. He looked a lot like Sammy lying there, except the bullet hole was in his chest instead of his forehead.

By the time the cops had gone through Mac's house with a fine-tooth comb and given me the same treatment, it was dawn. Given Mac's reputation, I'd expected to see Buchalter, but he must have been busy.

As I watched the M.E.'s boys wheel the body out, I wondered if Cy would recognize Mac when they got him on the table. Then I wondered if they planned to resurrect him, and if so, if anyone would take the job.

Nobody offered me a ride anywhere, which was okay since I didn't want anybody knowing where I was going. If I told the cops what I was thinking before I had proof, they'd lock me up and use me for batting practice.

The lack of light in the Blish Building didn't bother me this time any more than the cheap lock somebody had latched on the front door. In an hour or so this part of downtown would be crawling with immigrants on their way to work or setting up folding tables to sell cheap European watches to cheap tourists, but right now it was deserted.

There was no reason to be quiet walking down the hall this time. The vamps were all sleeping it off somewhere, and the zombies had wandered away to wherever they spent their few precious days. Didn't their families wonder what they were doing all night?

The blinds in the office had been drawn tight, which I

thought was just as well. I flipped on the overhead lights while I rounded the desk, intending to search the drawers. Maybe Angie had left a note, or a phone number.

"Well, what do you know?" I said. "Finally I catch a break."

What Angie had left in the office—was Angie. He was lying on the floor behind the desk. There were faint cuts and bruises on still visible on his face and neck. Apparently Leonard wasn't as puffy as I'd supposed.

It wasn't that far past daybreak; I shook him, not gently.

"Angie. Angie, wake up!"

His eyes fluttered and his nose flared. "Hey, man, you smell good. Back for—?" His eyes opened long enough to see me. "Oh, hell!"

I'm sure my smile wasn't a nice smile. It wasn't meant to be.

"You need to stay awake, Angie, because we're going to have a talk. You're going to tell me how you get your zombies. If you tell me the truth, I won't walk over there and let some light into this room."

Angelo was awake now, but during the day he was weak as a kitten. I had him cold and he knew it.

"You—um—okay, okay. What do I care what you meat-sacks do to each other, right?"

Now maybe sometimes I know what's coming because I'm psychic, and maybe sometimes it's because I'm a detective—but this time it was because I heard the door to the file room open.

I started to turn, but Angelo could see what was happening before I could, and his mouth opened at the same instant one of the window blinds shot upward, letting in the sunlight and cutting off his scream before it could start. A flash of sunlight, and that was all there was for

Angie. I blinked at Sammy's killer.

"Hey, Cy, how'd your date go the other night?"

"Fine. We went to dinner. And a motion picture. Gary Cooper."

"Sounds like fun." I casually stood up, keeping my hands in the clear. Cy's grip on his Police Special was too steady for comfort. "You know, you almost had me fooled. At first I thought Mac killed Sammy, because Angelo said his source wasn't picky about where he got the bodies. But the trouble with that was these zombies were all just regular joes looking for a little more time. Mac did specialty work. This kind of assembly-line resurrection wasn't his style. And who could supply that many bodies easier than a morgue attendant? A morgue attendant who suddenly had cash to burn."

"There's nothin' illegal about me getting a resurrection license. And I just picked out the ones nobody wanted. I gave 'em a few extra days. They were glad I did it."

"Sure, when you told them how if they went to a certain vamp club downtown and left the vamps suck out the blood they didn't need anyway, they could last longer. But you lied to them. And then there was Sammy."

"Hell." He honestly looked sad. "Everybody's got a grapevine, you know? Private eyes, reporters, vampires... even zombies." He rolled his eyes. "Who knew? Somebody told Sammy about the club, and he came in one night while I was here on business. Well, I knew right away *I* hadn't brought him in, so I figured I'd better follow him when he left, and he went straight to your office. If he'd told you what was goin' on, you'd have queered the deal."

"And Mac?"

Cy smiled. "Mac. Mac was a stroke of luck. When you said he might be able to raise Sammy, I had to get rid of him. But I didn't know..." he stopped to breathe deeply, savoring his own cleverness. "There is so much magic in that guy that when I raise him, he'll be worth a fortune to the vamps. You, not so much. But still worth it. A nice bonus for having to come down here before dawn to talk to that idiot Angelo."

Nice to know my death would benefit somebody, since I'd never bothered with life insurance.

"By the way," Cy said, grinning. "You'll like this." He hefted the Police Special. "This is Buchalter's gun. I'm gonna leave here where the cops'll find it."

"I gotta tell you, Cy, even as a zombie, I'll keep my free will." It was a small room; if he didn't stop me with the first bullet I might have a chance to grab the gun. "I won't let the vampires have me."

He snorted. "They're vampires. They've got twice the strength of a living man, let alone a zombie."

"There's a lot you don't know about zombies, Cy."

"And there is even more he doesn't know about raising the dead."

Mac the Life stood in the doorway. He was dead, but he didn't look it.

Cy jerked the gun in Mac's direction. I thought I saw his hand shaking.

"You can't be back. I never touched you!" He looked at me, but I just shook my head. Not me...

Mac mirrored my headshake. "You're an idiot, Cy. You don't know half as much as *he* does, and he doesn't know half of what I do. I set up my own resurrection spell a long time ago. You didn't know you could do that, did you?" He pointed at me. "Then I just followed him. I knew he'd find you."

Mac lunged with a speed I'd never seen in a zombie. Cy shot him twice in the chest, but Mac just kept coming until he got his hands on the gun. They struggled, there was another shot, and they both fell, dead for the first and last time.

I slumped into a chair, reached for the telephone, then stopped. I took Buchalter's gun from Cy's hand, wiped it off, and hid it where the cops would find it, just like Cy had planned.

For Sammy.

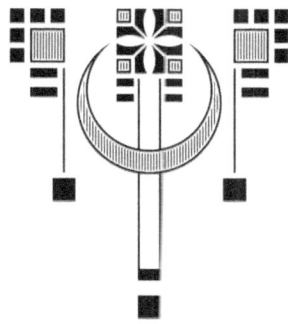

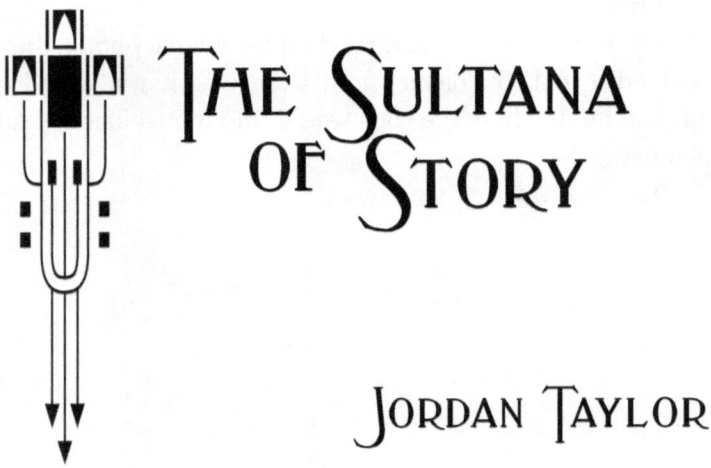

THE SULTANA OF STORY

JORDAN TAYLOR

"LISTEN," the Sultana says, "This is a ghost story."

She lights the dripping white candle on the little cloth-covered table in front of her, pushing her gauzy black veil away from her face. In the blooming light you can see her wide, dark eyes and the bruises underneath, her white hands floating in the dark like doves.

There had been the knot of a crowd in the street below the crumbling brick and twisted iron of her building, all shaggy bangs over their eyes and pants legs sweeping the ground and cigarettes held at their cocked hips like little smoking revolvers.

It was this that had arrested your attention, more so than the block-type letters of the sign hung out of her fifth-story window: MIND-READING, TAROT, AND PALMISTRY. SEE YOUR FUTURE! SEANCES THURSDAY EVENINGS AT SEVEN. Underneath was that staple of the New York City Psychic, the all-seeing eye.

No, anywhere a crowd gathers in New York something worth seeing is sure to be close by, this you have learned. It may not be what you have been searching for, but sometimes it is. That is the beauty of New York.

So you'd hung around, and when the crowd had entered the lobby of the building, scuffed and dirty marble under their feet, sagging tin ceiling, graffiti on the walls, and climbed the steep and narrow piss-smelling stairs, you had drifted along with them.

You stand in the back of the dusty little room, the better to see the Sultana but not be seen. You tug the brim of your hat down over your face.

The Sultana says: "When I was a child, I sold stories in the streets for a ha'penny.

"I'd been born a princess, in India, the spoiled only child of a rich, widowed officer. My mother was a native, dying in the bungalow of my father as she gave birth to his child. I was given to an ayah, was fed on the milk of the Ganges, on the sweet fruit of the mango and date. But after I was brought to my father's cold world of smoke and rain, my karma changed."

Her accent is strange, you notice that now, as if she has spoken a thousand languages and they are all trying to make themselves known on her tongue. It is impossible to tell how old she is. Her skin is lined, but her hair is still dark, dark under her veil, and she could be anywhere between forty and ninety.

"When my father died, the matron of my English boarding school took away my silks and my furs, my books and my lace. I was a pauper in the moment that it takes for the cobra to strike.

"In school I'd been famous for the stories I told. Now they were all I had.

"My father's ghost followed me through the gaslit streets when I ran errands for the cook, the mud seeping through the holes in my boots, wrapped his intangible arms around me when I shivered in my garret bed. *Once upon a time,* I whispered to him."

A draft of air stirs the candle's flame, and you shudder.

There is someone here—I feel her—It's a woman—who wants you to know that she forgives you, and though the Sultana is not looking at you, your hands shake and you step backwards until you can melt into the shadows dancing on the peeling yellow wallpaper.

"Once upon a time," the Sultana says, "My father's ghost entered the body of a monkey, and led me to the home of his former friend, whom had just returned from India.

"His friend took me in, and he dressed me in silks and furs and lace, and he put books in my hands, and Father's ghost smiled at me from the corner of the room, his transparent skin blistered and red from tropical fever, as the pet monkey he'd once lived in bared its teeth at me from its perch on the tall marble mantle.

"I called my father's friend 'The Gentleman,' because I was not a little girl anymore. He fed me on opium and told me to call him 'Uncle.'

"At night we dozed by the fire, our pipes hanging from our fingers, my father's ghost smiling broadly in the corner, and then I told them stories.

"Some were from my life. Some I made up. It was like the parlor game, two truths and a lie—Or is it two lies and a truth?—and The Gentleman could never guess."

The Sultana passes her thin hand over the candle-flame, idly, so that the room goes from pitch dark to dim again. The crowd that sits on the threadbare Persian carpet or stands, like you, in the shadowed corners shifts uncomfortably in their haze of incense and marijuana smoke. The Sultana raises her dark eyes to the room. "Would you like to play?"

"Once," the Sultana begins, "In India, a saw a young rajah carried through the dusty streets on the backs of ten men. He was so covered in gems that no one could look at him, but bent their faces to the ground.

"Once, when I was a servant, I saw a beggar child eaten by a dog. The dog, I think, did not know that the child was alive—it was only skin and bones, after all, and it lay in the doorway so still—but it met my eyes as I ran by.

"Once, when I was in school, my father sent me a doll the size of myself. She had me-sized evening gloves, and a me-sized opera glass, and a me-sized gown. And who, then, could say which of us was the doll?"

Does anyone have a cigarette? A girl in the front row shifts where she sits cross-legged on the floor, takes her pack out of her back pocket and passes one to the Sultana. The Sultana lights it on her candleflame, drawing on the smoke luxuriously as she watches the crowd with her dark eyes. A young man stands up in the back, makes as if to slip out while she is distracted. Oh, you don't believe in ghosts, sir? The Sultana laughs, her hands fluttering in the air, smoke dancing around her dark veil. No matter. They believe in you.

The Sultana drops her voice, a cigarette dangling from her white hand, and as one the crowd leans forward to listen.

She says: "I wore a jeweled turban to my first ball. The

Gentleman called me his harem girl. I'd danced as a child, in school, but that was several lifetimes ago, and in this incarnation I hardly knew how. The ball was full of officers, all trying to outdrink their deaths. I sat alone on the edges of the crowd, dazzled and longing for opium.

"A boy in uniform sat down beside me. The lights of the chandeliers glittered in his slicked back hair.

'You look like a Sultana,' he said, and my father's ghost, by the buffet, tossed back a drink.

"To be a Sultana was infinitely preferable to a harem girl, and so I smiled at him with one side of my mouth" —and she smiles that way now, so that just for a moment you can see what she looked like when she was young—"And I said, 'Once upon a time...'"

The Sultana's voice rises to fill the room. "Once upon a time, an enigmatic heiress was married to the war hero son of a prominent London family, and the wedding made all the papers. I walked down the aisle on the arm of my father's ghost, my eyes lined in kohl, as The Gentleman watched from the front pew, his arthritic fingers trembling on his jeweled cane.

"But I soon learned that marriage was only another kind of servitude. I left my husband in just a few short years, to travel to the Continent. My father's ghost leaned against the ship's railing and shook his head in dismay." The Sultana's lips quirk again.

"I joined the other *artistes* in Paris. I conducted seances, told stories, smoked with Zelda." She laughs a husky laugh and stubs out her cigarette on the shawl-covered table in front of her, as if daring the audience to cry "Bullshit."

"My father's ghost followed me from apartment to party, clearing his throat, frowning, this tiresome vestige of the last century, and I could not shake him. When he breathed on my neck I could feel again the tight laces of my dolls' clothes, the gnawing pain of starvation in my belly, the stifling heat of The Gentleman's fire, the numbness of my husband's war-hardened silence.

"We called it living fast, that mad champagne fizz between wars, and that was what it felt like, like I was running from the red-blistered face of death."

The Sultana's eyes are closed, the white spiders of her hands reaching for the room. Is there someone here whose name begins with R? Is there a Robert here? A Reggie? Her eyes fly open, her voice a hoarse gasp. Ralph?

"When the war came again," the Sultana says, "I took another ship to America. They were taking Jewish refugees, then, and I looked Jewish enough. A friend forged my papers and I spent all my life's savings on my ticket.

"I was Sara Crewe no longer, but Sarah Cronenberg." The Sultana drops her voice like a stone falling into the dark room. "Change your name and you change yourself.

"The ship was overcrowded—not even room for a ghost—and with my new identity I shook my father at last."

The Sultana raises her wrinkled arms, and the candleflame dances across the faces of the audience. "It was the land of freedom, of free free free, and when I landed I changed my name again, no more karma dogging my steps, I had taken it in my fists. Steam-set hair and my shirtsleeve rolled up over my bicep, I was in charge and I was one step ahead.

"I was Sarah Charkrabarti, Sultana of a new land, and I settled in New York and opened my own salon for immigrants, did my shopping in Chinatown, held seances in my apartment, the lease for which I'd signed myself in my new name."

The Sultana smiles and spreads her hands. In the candlelight her teeth are white as ghosts.

"And here I have been ever since. I will not say that I am everyone's granny, the psychic lady upstairs. I am much more than that.

"I am the last true psychic of New York City. I am the Sultana of Story, the Bodhisattva of Darkness, the Maharanee of the In-Between." Her eyes glow like dark coals, and the little boys and girls in the audience draw back, allowing you to glide through them to the front of the room as if through a sea of supplicants, their faces all pressed to the ground.

"I am the Rajimata of Unwanted Memories," the Sultana says, her voice huge in the dirty little apartment, "But I forgot that no one can escape their karma. Their death."

Her eyes fix on your face, pinning you in place like an infantry rifle's bayonet through the chest.

The boys and girls look around at one another, searching for who has caught her attention, but of course they see no one at all. You tip your tall, old fashioned hat to her with one blistered hand.

She smiles. "It seems mine has caught up with me at last."

Contributors

Marlin Bressi is the author of *Hairy Men in Caves: True Stories of America's Most Colorful Hermits* (Sunbury Press, 2015) and creator of the paranormal website *Journal of the Bizarre.* He was also the runner-up in the 2016 Milwaukee Paranormal Conference national horror fiction contest.

Goran Delic is a Concept Artist and Art Director with 20+ years experience in the entertainment industry for a variety of projects, including graphic novels, animation, editorial illustration and live action. www.gorandelic.com

Kevin Frost would like to live in the diesel powered oddity that is Scotty's Castle, but the National Park Service disagrees. He can often be found managing the *Curiosities* inbox while eating burritos (smothered, Christmas) at a lonely crossroads diner somewhere in northern New Mexico.

Eddie Generous is the author of the novel *Radio Run* (Severed Press 2018), the collection *Dead is Dead, but Not Always* (Hellbound Books 2018), and the novel *Camp Summit* (DBP 2019). He is the founder/editor/publisher/artist of **Unnerving** and *Unnerving Magazine,* and the host of the *Unnerving Podcast.* He lives on the Pacific Coast of Canada with his wife and their cat overlords. You can find out more at www.jiffypopandhorror.com

Brian K. Lowe has been writing since he was a child, the same time during which he was devouring comic books and travelling to Mars with Edgar Rice Burroughs. A graduate of UCLA, Brian lives in Southern California with his wife. He works as a paralegal in securities law. His SF trilogy, *The Stolen Future*, is available from Digital Fiction Publishing. Write to him at brianklowewriter@aol.com. He blogs at brianklowe.wordpress.com

Sebastien Mantle is a Canadian-born fantasy and sci-fi writer with a special place in his blackened heart for grimdark, and occasional silliness. Between novel-length projects, he churns out short stories ranging from bloody to ridiculous, and oftentimes both, all to the dulcet tones of whatever heavy metal band takes his fancy at the time.

Andrew McCurdy is a writer and editor whose day job as a Speech-Language Pathologist involves helping nonverbal, special needs children access technology to maximize their ability to communicate. He lives in rural Nova Scotia with an eleven-year-old girl, two ancient cats, and a brazen, little hamster named *Mouse*—who frequently (and magically) escapes the confines of her cage to taunt the tired, old cats with daring midnight runs across the kitchen floor.

Dimitra Nikolaidou is usually dreaming of forests. When awake, she is completing her PhD on roleplaying games and speculative fiction at the Aristotle University of Thessaloniki. She is the creative editor of Archetypo Publications, and teaches speculative creative writing at Tales of the Wyrd. Her stories have been included in various anthologies and magazines such as *Metaphorosis, See the Elephant, After the Happily Ever After,* and *Αντίθετο Ημισφαίριο.*

Manuel Royal, like Tristram Shandy, was born with a broken nose, followed by interminable digressions. Although his body resides in Atlanta, Georgia, his mind can be found shuffling down the alleys and circumnavigating the roundabouts of *Donnetown*, an imaginary midsize city somewhere in the Carolinas.
donnetowntoday.blogspot.com

Holly Schofield travels through time at the rate of one second per second, oscillating between the alternate realities of city and country life. Her short stories have appeared in *Analog, Lightspeed, Tesseracts,* and many other publications throughout the world. She hopes to save the world through science fiction and homegrown heritage tomatoes. Find her at hollyschofield.wordpress.com.

M. A. Smith writes from Gloucestershire, UK, where she lives with her family. Her fiction has appeared in magazines including *Mythic, Gathering Storm* and *Dark Moon Digest,* and her novella *Severance* was published by Fantasia Divinity earlier this year. Find out more at www.masmithwriting.com.

Jordan Taylor has driven across the US three times, and lived in four different cities in as many years. She currently resides in Seattle, Washington, with her husband, their corgi, and too many books for one small apartment. Her short fiction has recently appeared in or is forthcoming from *On Spec* and *Beneath Ceaseless Skies.* You can follow her online at jordanrtaylor.com.

DJ Tyrer has been published in *Chilling Horror Short Stories* (Flame Tree), *Steampunk Cthulhu* (Chaosium), and *EOM: Equal Opportunity Madness* (Otter Libris), and issues of *Hinnom Magazine, Ravenwood Quarterly,* and *Weirdbook,* and in addition, has a novella available in paperback and on the Kindle, *The Yellow House* (Dunhams Manor).

THIS IS HOW THE WORLD ENDS. NOT WITH A BOMB
BUT BY *SOCIAL MEDIA*

THE
MACHINE
STOPS

BY C. M. FORSTER

AVAILABLE
NOW AT YOUR
PUBLIC DOMAIN ARCHIVE

Questa Grande has
gadzooks which Scribus
would not render.
curiousgallery
@gmail.
com

www.ingramcontent.com/pod-product-compliance
Lightning Source LLC
Chambersburg PA
CBHW022025170626
46808CB00003B/1068